For Love of a Horse

Patricia Leitch started riding when a friend persuaded her to go on a pony trekking holiday – and by the following summer she had her own Highland pony, Kirsty. She wrote her first book shortly after this and writing is now her full-time occupation, but she has also done all sorts of different jobs, including being a riding-school instructor, groom, teacher and librarian. She lives in Renfrewshire, Scotland, with a bearded collie called Meg.

'Jinny' series

For Love of a Horse
A Devil to Ride
The Summer Riders
Night of the Red Horse
Gallop to the Hills
Horse in a Million
The Magic Pony
Ride Like the Wind
Chestnut Gold
Jump for the Moon
Horse of Fire

Patricia Leitch

For Love of
a Horse

An Original Armada

For Love of a Horse was first published in Armada in 1976
This impression 1991

Armada is an imprint of
the Children's Division, part of
HarperCollins Publishers Ltd,
77–85 Fulham Palace Road,
Hammersmith, London W6 8JB

Printed and bound in Great Britain by
HarperCollins Book Manufacturing, Glasgow

CHAPTER ONE

It all happened suddenly. In a three. The way things do.

"But that's rubbish," thought Jinny, pressing her forehead against the cold glass of the window pane. "It only seems like that to us. Billions and millions and trillion billions of things all happened. We just picked three of them."

She stared down at the busy Stopton street opposite their flat – at the supermarket, the dress shop and the Bingo Hall. In her ears was the growling throb of constant traffic. Throughout all her eleven years, Jinny had never lived anywhere else but in the city. Even at two in the morning the traffic roared and pounded in the street outside their home. All night long, footsteps rang sharp on the pavements. This was the way you lived, caged in by noise – a human sardine packed in with all the others. If you were lucky, you went away for a fortnight in the summer to the country, but that wasn't the way you lived – that was holidays. The city was your real life.

Then, suddenly, the three things happened. Whizz, crash, bang – and tonight was their last night in Stopton. Tomorrow the Manders family were going to live in the Highlands of Scotland. In a grey stone house, Finmory House, that had its own beach, Finmory Bay, its own moors, and even its own mountain, Finmory Beag.

They had looked it up on an Ordnance Survey map in Stopton Library.

"That's our house," Mike had said to the library assistant who came to wag a fat finger at them and point to the SILENCE notice.

"And none of your lies either," she had told him, not believing their wish come true.

"But it *is* true," Jinny breathed. "True tomorrow. Tomorrow night we'll be in Inverburgh, and the next night – Finmory."

Jinny's breath steamed the window pane. She breathed harder, then wrote with her finger nail:

Horses
Ponies
Foals

She stood back from the window to gaze for a second, entranced by the spell she had cast.

"Horses, ponies and foals. Oh my!" she chanted, in a *Wizard of Oz* tune. "Horses, ponies and foals. Oh my!"

For a moment longer, she stood without moving, then she swung away from the window, her mane of straight, red-gold hair flying out from her head, her blue eyes bright with excitement, her wide mouth stretching her sharp, small-featured face into nothing but grin.

"Horses, ponies and foals. Oh my!" she yelled, as she pranced through their flat. "Horses, ponies and foals. Oh my!" Her bare, bony feet stamped out the rhythm as she went dancing through the rooms where she had always lived – and after tomorrow would never see again.

Mr. Manders, packing the last of his books into tea chests, paused and shouted to Jinny to make less noise or old Mrs. Robertson would be banging on the ceiling again. He was a short, thick-set man, with shoulder-length hair that was wearing bald on top, a thick, reddish beard and a face that crinkled into long laughter lines. Really, he was glad that one of his family could plunge into the thought of their new life with such total enthusiasm. Now that the decision had actually been taken, Mr. Manders was wondering desperately if he was doing the right thing. A middle-aged Stopton probation officer suddenly selling up everything and going off to the Highlands. He was going to write a book and be a potter. At one time, the fact that the only pottery Mr. Manders had ever done in his life had been at evening classes had only made the move seem more of an adventure. But during the last month he had been waking up in the early hours of the morning to lie staring into the darkness, wondering if it was all a mad nonsense. He told himself he had no choice. He had reached the stage where he had to go. He couldn't bear the hopelessness of being a probation officer in a big city for a moment longer.

Mrs. Manders and Petra were in the kitchen, wrapping up dishes in sheets of newspaper.

"Watch what you're doing," Mrs. Manders warned, as Jinny's elbow knocked a mug off a shelf. But because she was high with excitement, poised on the knife edge of a new life, Jinny's hand flashed out, caught the mug before it crashed to the floor, and put it back safely on the table.

"You'll end in tears," Petra warned – as if she were fifty, not fourteen. Jinny stuck her tongue out at her without interrupting her chant. "And don't be so childish," Petra snapped.

Petra had short, brown, curly hair like her mother's. Without much washing she stayed clean and tidy. Dirt seemed to fly away from Petra as readily as it seemed drawn to Jinny. When Petra knotted a scarf around her neck, it stayed where Petra put it, its ends twisted attractively, like the scarves in the women's magazines that Petra was always reading. When Jinny tried to improve her appearance by knotting one of Petra's scarves fashionably round her neck, people kept on asking if she had a sore throat. Petra played the piano. She practised every night, working endlessly at scales and exercises. She passed all the exams she sat and was going to be a music teacher. Jinny was tone deaf, but it seemed to her that Petra couldn't play at all. It was all work – not music. If Jinny had been musical, as Petra was supposed to be, she would never have wanted to be a music teacher. She would have been a soloist, playing to vast, silent audiences all over the world, their applause flaming around her and going on for ever.

"Horses, ponies and foals," chanted Jinny, seeing calm bay hunters, shaggy Highland ponies, woolly foals with bottle-brush tails and perhaps, perhaps, the horse of Jinny's dreams – an Arab mare who would come cantering over the moors when Jinny called her name.

"Have you packed your painting things yet?" her mother asked.

Jinny shook her head.

"Well, you won't let me near them, so if you don't do it I suppose they'll be left here."

Jinny supposed her mother was right, and, finding scissors and a ball of string, she went through to her bedroom to get on with it.

Mike was sitting on her bed, reading.

"Mind your legs," Jinny said, and crouched down to bring out her boxes from under the bed. She hardly ever let any of her family see her drawings. If they did see them, they always said the wrong things. Even when they praised them, they still said the wrong things. But Mike didn't count.

There were three flat cardboard boxes, overflowing with paintings and drawings, and a folder filled with work from school that Miss Dickson had allowed her to keep when school had broken up last week for the summer holidays.

"Now, whatever else you do in this wilderness that your mad father is taking you to, don't you dare stop drawing, Jinny Manders," Miss Dickson had said as she sat at her desk taking a last look at Jinny's paintings.

"No, Miss Dickson."

"Get a cardboard box."

Jinny had brought a box from the shelf at the back of the classroom, and Miss Dickson had taken her into the walk-in cupboard where none of the class was ever allowed to go.

"Now hold that up and let's see what we can find for you."

Jinny had held the box while Miss Dickson had filled it with plastic tubes of poster paint, most of them almost empty, but some still half full. She had dropped in a new box of pastels, a tin of used wax crayons, four black felt-tipped pens, two thick paint brushes and a paint-encrusted palette. "You can clean that up for yourself. Vim, hot water and elbow grease." Then she had reached up to the top shelf, lifted down a thick wad of drawing paper and laid it on top of the box. "Now, remember, don't you dare stop painting."

"For me!" Jinny had gasped in astonishment.

Miss Dickson had nodded, and marched out of the cupboard before Jinny had even begun to thank her.

Jinny stretched under the bed, wriggling to reach the box at the furthermost corner. She dragged it out and examined her treasures. She felt like a miser fingering her gold. The thick, squidgy tubes of paint, the prim row of brand-new pastels, the cough sweet tin full of shiny bits of wax crayon, and the thick brushes. Jinny spat on the palette, rubbed one of the brushes into it, and tried the effect of saliva and mud-coloured paint along the edge of a sheet of paper.

"You're not starting to paint now?" asked Mike, shutting his book and stretching out on his front, with his face hanging over the edge of the bed as he watched his sister.

"'Course not," said Jinny. "I'm packing them up." And she began to sort the drawings and paintings into piles.

All the animals that Jinny had been able to find in the city were in her drawings, but mostly they were of horses. There were the ponies who still pulled the carts through the city traffic, some plump and well cared for, but some galled and rheumy-eyed. There were police horses, who always seemed to Jinny to be almost a part of the policemen's uniform. Despite their shining tack and well-shod hooves, Jinny couldn't help feeling that nobody loved them. Once, coming home with her family very late on a Sunday night, they had seen a young policeman riding a black horse and leading a bay, galloping them along the deserted street. Jinny looked at her painting of the two galloping police horses, the young man and the high, gloomy buildings. It wasn't very good – the policeman's arms were wrong – but the two horses were alive, being horses again instead of hairy Z-cars.

Most of the drawings of people riding were of pupils from Major Young's riding school. It cost two pounds for an hour's ride. Now and again, Jinny had saved up enough birthday and Christmas money to have two pound notes to give to Major Young. He didn't approve of children who arrived in jeans. Incorrect dress, he called it, and kept Jinny out of sight, tucked away in a back paddock, bumping round and round on a stolid, dark brown cob. "Don't come again until you're properly kitted out," the Major would tell her. But it was such a long time between Jinny's riding lessons that the Major had always forgotten her.

Jinny leafed through her drawings of correctly-dressed riding school pupils. Fat, scared girls, clutching their reins in gloved hands; boys who were bored; chatting ladies who looked as if they should have had their knitting with them, and a superior girl who stabled her showjumpers with Major Young.

"The city's not the place for horses," Jinny thought. "But Finmory will be." And Jinny was swamped by the thought that tomorrow she would have left Stopton for ever; that it was true; that it was real. Sea and mountains and a Highland pony to ride.

"It did happen in a three, didn't it?" she said to Mike.

Mike held up two fingers and a thumb. He was nine, brown-eyed and curly-haired like Petra, but easy company, always pleased to be with you.

"Granny Manders died," he said and tucked down his thumb.

Granny Manders had been eighty-nine and as small as Jinny, her long wisp of white hair always carefully arranged round her pink scalp. High lace collars matched the crêpe skin of her neck, and enormous rings weighted her dry, bony fingers. She had lived with a Miss Simpson in an echoing house full of shadows, oil portraits and mice. She had died in her sleep.

"Two," said Mike. "Daddy sold her house. And three, he packed in being a probation officer. Hey, that's nice." He tried to pick up a pencil drawing of one of the shire horses that pulled the brewers' drays. Jinny whisked it out of his reach and packed it away in a box.

"Why did Dad stop? So suddenly, I mean?" Mike asked.

Jinny wasn't quite sure herself. "Remember Paula Hay?"

Mike screwed up his face. Dimly, he thought he could remember a spotty girl who had giggled a lot. So many of the people Mr. Manders had worked with, and tried to help, had come to their house over the years that they were mixed in Mike's memory.

"Uh, huh," he said vaguely.

"Well, I think," said Jinny, tying up her boxes, "that it was because of her. They sent her to prison because there was no room for her anywhere else. Dad couldn't stop them. She wasn't much older than Petra."

10

"What had she done?"

"Stolen food from a super. That was the last thing she did. Done other things before that."

Jinny pulled the string tightly around her box, knotting it hard. She didn't want to think too much about Paula Hay. She had overheard her mother and father talking about her when Mr. Manders had come home from the court that had sent Paula to prison. If it wasn't so impossible that it could never, never be true, Jinny would have thought her father had been crying. Once, Jinny had gone with her father to the two rooms where the Hays lived. There had been a baby that looked like a wizened old man, who had cried all the time they were there with a thin, whining noise, and four other children lying in a bed under a blanket that was black with dirt. The smell had choked in Jinny's throat for days afterwards, and the baby still haunted her dreams.

"We won't see Ken again," said Mike regretfully.

"No," said Jinny, tugging harder than ever at her knots. Ken was another thing that she wasn't too keen on thinking about. Ken had been magic. He would have been looking for a winged horse at Finmory, not just an Arab. When Jinny had shown Ken her drawings, he had known what to say. And once he had arrived outside their flat, like a miracle, with a skewbald pony, saddled and bridled, and taken Jinny for a ride through Stopton. His probation had ended over three months ago, and since then they hadn't seen him again. As long as they stayed in Stopton, Jinny was always expecting to open the door and find Ken there. But how would he possibly find them at Finmory?

"Want to see my surprise?" asked Mike.

He led the way to his bedroom, opened his empty wardrobe, and three kittens came fumbling, delicate-pawed, on to the carpet.

"Finmory cats," said Mike. "There were only three left in the pet shop so she gave them to me."

Jinny picked up the black kitten. Its needle claws caught in her shirt. Tiny triangles of ears pricked upright above the flower face. It pushed its head against her hand, twitching its ridiculous scrap of tail.

"They're the first," said Jinny. "Our very first animals."

"Supper's ready," called Mrs. Manders. "Come and get it."

But Jinny hardly heard her. "The very first," she repeated, and trooping out of the open wardrobe came dogs and a goat, ducks and hens and all the wild animals that were at Finmory, waiting for them. The animals that Jinny had been longing for all her life were there, but best of all was the promise of ponies. Jinny saw Palominos and Appaloosas, Norwegian ponies, Exmoors and Highlands, retired racehorses, pensioned-off carthorses and rescued donkeys, all grazing together.

"Horses, ponies and foals. Oh my!" she breathed.

And, not tomorrow but the next day, they would all start to come true.

CHAPTER TWO

The removal men banged on the door at seven the next morning, and in less than two hours, all the furniture was packed into the van, leaving bare boards – and wallpaper surprisingly bright where wardrobes and bedheads had kept it from fading.

It wasn't home any longer.

"Oh, come on, come on," Jinny muttered under her breath, as everyone gathered in the kitchen for a last cup of tea before setting off. Jinny couldn't bear to stay. She hated this terrible, lost time when she belonged nowhere – was left floating with nothing to hold on to. "If the wind of God came now," Jinny thought, "we would all be blown away like dust. I'm not the Jinny Manders who lived here, but who I'm going to be I don't know."

"Oh, come on, come on," Jinny muttered more loudly, making her father scowl at her and Petra drink her tea more slowly.

At last the boss removal man stood up. "Better be off," he said. "Got a tidy way to go."

Mr. Manders was going with the removal van, waiting while the furniture was unloaded at Finmory, then coming back to Inverburgh where, hopefully, Mrs. Manders and the children would be installed at the Gordon Hotel. They were all spending the night there, then driving on to Finmory the next morning.

Mike and Jinny waved goodbye to the van, then ran back upstairs to where Petra and their mother were packing last-minute things into carrier bags.

"I can smell those kittens already," moaned Petra.

Mike suggested a clothes peg for Petra's nose, but removed the basket of kittens and rushed them down to the back seat of the Rover. Mrs. Manders had not been overjoyed when she had found them the night before, and Mike wasn't risking a return visit to the pet shop on their way north.

"Now, do you think we've remembered everything?" Mrs. Manders said as they all stood at the front door.

"Everything. Absolutely everything," Jinny assured her.

"Don't rush me," said her mother. "This is our final exit."

Mike did a jet tour, running from empty room to empty room.

"Not even a Manders' flea left," he reported.

"Right, then. This is it." And Mrs. Manders closed the door with a bang.

They packed bags into the already overflowing boot and climbed in the car. Petra in front, Mike and Jinny with the kittens in the back.

As Mrs. Manders started up the engine, Jinny looked back at the blank, curtainless windows. For a moment, she thought she saw someone move, but it was only a shadow. "It might have been myself," she thought wildly. "Myself watching me go." And she twisted round, staring out through the windscreen, staring towards Scotland and the North.

They drove through the centre of the city that they all knew so well, on between rows and rows of crumbling, brick terrace houses and then through the lush Stopton suburbs, until Mrs Manders turned on to the boredom of the motorway. She drove steadily on the inside lane. On and on they went. Drugged by the flash of passing cars and the glimmering, whale's back ribbon of road, Jinny's eyes closed. She woke gritty and cross. Next to her, Mike was still asleep, and Petra was telling her mother some

13

long, involved story about Pamela Cook being so rude to Miss Berry.

"Are we nearly there?" asked Jinny, but no one bothered to answer her.

When they stopped for lunch, the hillsides were furred with forestry pine trees, and, far ahead of them, Jinny could see the faint, half-imagined bulk of mountains, pale grey and dusk purple, rearing up into the sky. She breathed in gulps of clear, sharp air.

"Can't you feel it?" she demanded. "It smells quite different to Stopton."

"What?" said Petra.

"Scotland, of course," said Jinny scornfully.

"Don't talk nonsense," said Petra. "We're still in England."

"But I can feel it blowing down to meet us. Eagles and pine trees and lochs."

"Never mind being blown down on," said her mother impatiently. "Eat up those sandwiches or it's going to be the middle of the night before we reach Inverburgh."

But it wasn't. They got there just before six, and after two misdirections found their way to the Gordon Hotel. Inside it was dark, with stags' heads on the walls and tartan carpets on the stairs.

"All the way from Stopton!" said the girl at the reception desk, as if they had come from the other end of the earth.

By the time Mr. Manders arrived, they had all washed, eaten every scrap of food that had been left in the picnic basket, and were slowly starving to death in the lounge.

"How did it go?" asked Mrs. Manders. "What's it like?"

Only Mr. Manders had seen Finmory before, and that had been three years ago.

He spread out his hands and rolled his eyes ceilingwards. Without speaking, he sank on to the settee next to his wife.

"Did the van break down?" demanded Petra.

"The doors opened and you've lost all the furniture?" guessed Mike.

"No," said their father. "We got there O.K."

14

"What's it like?" repeated Mrs. Manders suspiciously.

"Vast. Vaster than vast. I've phoned the Post Office to fix up an internal phone system."

"Oh no!" cried Mrs. Manders.

"Joy!" cried Jinny.

"We'll need to wear identification discs," Mr. Manders said seriously. "It's quite on the cards that we won't meet each other for months once we move in."

"It's not really as bad as that," said Petra.

"Nothing within miles. Only a farmhouse. Total isolation."

"I don't believe you," stated Mrs. Manders. "And I don't intend to believe you until I see it for myself."

Mr. Manders laughed. "Well, it is larger than I remembered," he said, and led the way into the dining room.

Mike was finishing his second helping of trifle when Mr. Manders looked at his watch.

"Pity you're all so worn out after your journey," he said.

"I'm not," said Mike instantly.

"Nor me," said Jinny.

"If you weren't all longing to get to bed I did happen to notice that there's a circus on just outside Inverburgh."

"Oh yes," cried Jinny and Mike. "Yes, let's."

Mrs. Manders and Petra settled down in the lounge to watch the colour television, while Jinny, Mike and their father drove to the outskirts of Inverburgh, where a big top was pitched on a stretch of waste ground.

The air was filled with grinding fairground music and the shouting voices of the crowds jostling around the stalls and amusements.

"Bumper cars?" pleaded Mike. "Oh, please, Dad?"

"Not if you want to see the circus," said Mr. Manders. "It starts in five minutes."

"The circus, the circus," insisted Jinny, jumping up and down on the muddy, crushed grass.

They went across to where a clown banging a drum was wearily urging people to hurry along to the greatest show on earth. Mr. Manders bought three tickets, and followed his children through the opening in the flapping canvas. A woman in a spangled costume showed them to their seats in the second row.

15

"You don't want popcorn. You've just finished a big meal," exclaimed Mr. Manders, but already Jinny had pushed her way out into the passage and was buying three bags.

"You need it for a circus, for crunching when they're on the high wire and catching each other on the trapezes," she explained, when she brought the popcorn back.

"Well, sit at the end," her father told her. "Don't come squeezing past us again."

He was beginning to wonder if the circus had been the brightest of ideas. The last circus the Manders had attended had been Billy Smart's, but already it was obvious that this one wasn't going to be quite the same. Under the clown's make-up, Mr. Manders had been able to see all too clearly the tired face of an old man, and beneath the woman's spangles her costume had been a soiled grey.

Jinny crunched her popcorn and the band crashed to a crescendo. The ringmaster strutted in, cracked his whip, announced the first act and the Jet Setters came into the ring.

Mr. Manders watched in embarrassment as they missed easy catches, fumbled simple routines and failed to balance even one plate on the end of a spinning pole. The applause that followed them out of the ring was a weak wash of sound that died almost before it had begun. The dogs, clowns and acrobats who followed them were all equally poor. Jinny clapped her hands almost raw in an effort to make more noise. At the interval she bought more popcorn. "Not for excitement," she explained, handing out second helpings. "Just to stop it being so awful."

"Want to go?"

"No," said Mike. "There might be lions."

Fervently, Mr. Manders prayed that there would not be lions.

"There's bound to be horses," said Jinny hopefully. "Perhaps they'll be better."

The horses were the last act, and, to Mr. Mander's relief, there hadn't been lions.

Two aged white rosinbacks cantered heavily around the ring while the ringmaster flicked their sunken quarters with the lash of his whip. The spangled lady who had

16

shown them to their seats stood insecurely with one foot on each broad back. Now and again she clapped her hands and cried, "Hoop la!" in a shrill voice.

Jinny gritted her teeth. She wished that the circus was over and they could go back to the hotel. She was sitting close enough to the ring to be able to see every detail of the horses – their patient, watery eyes, the harsh bits pulling back their lips, their scarred legs and sunken necks. One of them was broken-winded, and the harsh sound of its breathing tightened Jinny's throat. She hated the ringmaster, hated his pleated lips and beady, watching eyes. She flinched under the crack of his whip as if it stung against her own skin.

"And now, ladies and gentlemen," the ringmaster announced, as the two horses went out of the ring, "a final, special attraction. For the first time under canvas we present to you – Yasmin, the Killer Horse. Death lurks in her flying hooves. Tonight, at great personal risk, I have decided to allow her to make her first public appearance."

Jinny heard her father groan and stir irritably in his seat.

"All the way from Arabia – Yasmin, the Killer Horse."

Drum beats drowned his voice, and into the ring galloped a rich-chestnut mare with a white blaze and four white stockings. Jinny gasped with a sharp intake of breath, felt her scalp creep and a sudden coldness clamp down her spine.

The horse was a pure-bred Arab. She came, bright and dancing, flaunting into the ring, her tail held high over her quarters, her silken mane flowing over the crest of her neck. Her head was fine-boned and delicate, with the concave line of the true Arab horse. Her dark, lustrous eyes were fringed with long lashes and the nostrils wrinkling her velvet muzzle were huge black pits. She moved around the ring like a bright flame, her pricked ears delicate as flower petals. Her legs were clean and unblemished and her small hooves were polished ivory. After the dull ache of the rosinbacks, she was all light and fire.

Jinny sat entranced, hardly breathing, and then her breath burst out of her in a throbbing gasp. She loved the chestnut mare. As if all their long day's travelling had only been for this. As if she had come all the way from Stop-

17

ton only for this, to see this sudden gift of perfection.

Mr. Manders glanced at his daughter and felt his heart tighten with fear at what the future must hold for her, for she would always allow herself to love too deeply, and always suffer for it.

Suddenly, the ringmaster's whip cracked down on the chestnut's shoulders. Not the flickering sting he had used on the white horses, but a lash with the full force of his body behind it.

"No!" cried Jinny. "No!"

The chestnut reared. Her forefeet slashed the air like razors. Then she turned on the man, her neck low and snaking. Again he lashed her, and again she reared up.

"No!" screamed Jinny. "Stop it!"

Before her father realised what was happening, Jinny had jumped up from her seat, flung herself over the low barrier, dashed across the ring and thrown herself at the ringmaster.

"Don't you dare whip her! Don't you dare!" Jinny cried, grappling with the man, struggling to pull the whip out of his hand, kicking against his booted legs with her sandshoes.

For a second, the ringmaster was taken completely by surprise. Just long enough for the chestnut to gallop past them and out of the ring. The audience, thinking it was all part of the act, clapped with more enthusiasm than they had shown during the rest of the night.

The ringmaster gripped Jinny by the scruff of her anorak and shook her furiously. The band began to play the National Anthem, and the tiered rows of people pulsed slowly into the passages and began to make their way out of the tent.

Mr. Manders went to claim his daughter.

"That's enough," he said abruptly when the ringmaster, his face puce with fury, began to swear at him. "I don't know what the R.S.P.C.A. would have to say about your whole set-up, but it strikes me that they might be interested." And he turned, putting his arm round Jinny's shoulder, and steered her out of the ring.

"But couldn't you buy her instead of a Highland pony?" Jinny pleaded from the back of the car. "Oh, Daddy, please. She can't stay in that terrible circus. She can't."

"The Highlands are to take you to school. You couldn't ride that wild horse. You know that perfectly well. So don't, Jinny. Stop it now," said Mr. Manders.

"She's only young. I don't suppose anyone has tried to break her in gently. She's not wild. She shouldn't be in a circus. That brute of a man whipping her."

"You can't do anything about it, Jinny. There's nothing you can do." And Mr. Manders shut his ears against his daughter's pleading.

"Nothing you can do about it," he thought bitterly. But as he drove back to the Gordon, he wasn't thinking about horses that shouldn't be in circuses, but about the families he had worked with in Stopton. People who lived in decaying, overcrowded, rat-infested rooms and the kids who roamed the streets because there was nowhere for them to go – neither in the evenings, nor in life.

"She what?" exclaimed Petra. "She ran into the ring and kicked the ringmaster! Oh, you didn't!"

Jinny scowled at her sister.

"Long past 'time for bed'," said Mrs. Manders.

Jinny lay on her back in the narrow hotel bed. Tears drained into her throat. She saw in her mind's eye the chestnut mare flowing round the dingy circus ring, bright and burning, and she thought how the Arab should be free to gallop over the open land at Finmory. What was the point of there being open moors and hillsides if she had always to think of the chestnut being whipped round the circus ring, boxed from one stopping place to another until she became soured and vicious, or, even worse, broken and hopeless like the white rosinbacks?

CHAPTER THREE

"Finmory is over there," said Mr. Manders, pointing through the car window to where green hillsides, scarred with grey outcrops of rock, sheered up from the road.

"You mean we stop the car and climb?" asked his wife incredulously.

"Could do. Probably get there quicker. We stick to the main road for another four miles, then strike off to the left along a road that eventually brings you back to the other side of these hills."

Jinny put her head down on her knees. She could just manage to catch a glimpse of blue sky above the hills.

"Should Mike and I get out and walk over?" Jinny asked hopefully, imagining Mike and herself standing silhouetted on the very top of the hillside, staring down on Finmory, being the first to see their new home.

"No," refused her mother automatically. "Most certainly not."

Packed in the back of the car, the three children were tense with anticipation. They seemed to have been waiting for so long to see Finmory, and now they were nearly there.

"Couldn't you drive just a little bit faster?" suggested Mike. "You're going like a funeral."

"We'd *be* a funeral if I put on any speed. This is a filthy bit of road. Bad enough, I should have thought, when there was only local people using it – but now there's all these blasted tankers and lorries on it, it's nothing but a death trap. I'll stick to thirty, thank you very much."

They turned off on the road that led to Finmory. It went through Glenbost village, which was only six or seven whitewashed crofts scattered about the roadside, one sell-everything shop, two petrol pumps almost submerged under the rusted wrecks of old cars, and two churches – one painted green, with its corrugated iron roof tied on with rope.

"That's your new school," Mr. Manders said to Mike and Jinny, pointing out a stone building.

"Cor!" exclaimed Mike. "It's only one room!"

"And the schoolmaster's house attached," said Mr. Manders. "Probably only be about a dozen pupils."

"You mean we'll be in the same class?" demanded Jinny. School in Stopton had been a modern building made of plate glass and concrete. "I'll be in the same room as Mike?"

"Doesn't look up to much," said Petra smugly. She was too old for Glenbost School and would be going to Duninver Grammar School, staying in the school hostel during the week.

"In the same class as my brother," said Jinny in disgust as she stared uncertainly through the back window. Although she was very grateful not to have to stay in a hostel, she had never thought of a school with only one room in it. A tall, hook-nosed man with a red face and bald head had come to the schoolhouse door and was watching their car. Instantly, Jinny disliked him.

"D'you think that's the teacher?" she asked Mike, but by the time Mike had looked round the man had gone inside again.

They rattled over a cattle grid and followed the track over bleak moorland.

"But there's nothing," said Mrs. Manders. "Not a thing."

"Sheep," said Mike.

At the far edge of the moorland, mountains shouldered up against the sky. Cloud shadows raced over them so that their colours seemed to flow and change as you watched – deep purple turned to blue that faded into bleached pinks and mauves. Waterfalls streaked black gorges with threads of brilliant white as they crashed down the mountains' sides, and patches of dried moss were a vivid saffron gold. Ravens croaked, disturbed by the car, and two buzzards flew up from the telephone wires that followed the road.

"Oh, honestly, Tom," said Mrs. Manders. "Really!"

The track turned and dropped down to a farm, half-hidden in a clump of pine trees.

"We'll come back later for milk and eggs," said Mr. Manders. "That's the farmer, Mr. Mackenzie," he added, as a man driving a tractor in one of the fields by the farm waved to them. "Nearly there now."

The car crawled slowly along a muddy, rutted track, twisted through a broken-down gateway, and followed the overgrown drive that pushed its way between top-heavy, fungussy trees to Finmory House.

Mr. Manders stopped the car and flung himself back in his seat with a gesture of triumph. "We've made it," he shouted, pushing his splayed fingers through his beard. "Finmory, here we come."

21

They all burst out of the car to stand staring at the four-square, solid, stone house.

"It's smashing," breathed Mike.

"Sea at the bottom of the garden!" exclaimed Jinny. "And mountains peering down the chimneys."

"Looks terribly damp," said Mrs. Manders, laughing as her husband swung her round and kissed her.

"Huge," said Petra. "I'll be able to have Susan to stay."

"Why not?" agreed Mr. Manders, taking an enormous key from his pocket and setting it in the lock of the massive, iron-studded door. The lock turned with a groan worthy of a fairy-tale castle. Mr. Manders set his shoulder to the door and pushed it open.

Jinny dashed past him into a high, echoing hall. She stared into rooms full of dust and cobwebs, with windows that rattled in their frames when she opened the doors. The ceilings were decorated with crumbling plaster-work – so far above Jinny's head that she had to crane her neck back to see them properly. In two of the rooms their Stopton furniture huddled nervously together in the middle of the floor.

"But curtains," her mother said despairingly, as Jinny ran up the wide flight of stairs. "And carpets! Where will we ever find carpets?"

A corridor ran the length of the second floor. Its windows looked out towards the sea, and the doors of the bedrooms opened off it.

"Two bathrooms with absolutely antiquated loos," Mike yelled from further down the corridor.

Each bedroom opened on to a room decorated in a different colour.

"The yellow bedroom, the blue bedroom, the pink room, red room," Jinny shouted as she ran from one to the next.

At the end of the corridor, Jinny discovered an almost vertical ladder of stairs. She climbed up, opened the door at the top and found herself in a room divided into two parts by an archway. The window of the room on the left looked out to the sea.

"Mine," thought Jinny. "Mine."

Through to the other part of the room she ran, her feet leaving dark prints on the dusty floor. On one of the walls

22

was a mural of a chestnut horse. It was a red horse with yellow eyes that charged towards her through a growth of blue and green branches drooping under the weight of fleshy, white flowers.

Jinny heard steps coming up the stairs. She flew to the door.

"They're mine," she cried. "I've bagged them. These are my rooms."

Mrs. Manders and Petra stared at her in surprise.

"Don't panic," said Petra. "We're only coming to look."

"But these are attics, probably the servants' rooms at one time," said Mrs. Manders, looking at the low, sloping ceiling and seeing Jinny's mural as scribbling on the wall that would have to be painted over. "Are you sure this is the room you want for your bedroom?"

"Quite, quite, utterly positive," stated Jinny. "Quite, quite, utterly sure."

They had coffee, cheese sandwiches and apples, sitting in the kitchen with the kittens pouncing on their feet. The previous owners had left a long, oak table behind them.

"Shouldn't think they'd ever find another kitchen big enough for it," said Petra, looking around the room, which seemed almost as big as the whole of their Stopton flat put together.

"Right," said Mr. Manders, pushing back his chair, when they had all finished eating. "Working party fall in."

"I'm going up the hill," said Mike.

"Oh no you're not," said his father. "We'll all work until four. Then we'll all go out."

"But I'm ..."

"No buts."

Petra and Jinny did their best to clean out the kitchen. They scraped a growth of grease off the Aga, roused hairy Methusela spiders and black beetles from the corners under the sinks, tried to sweep the rush matting –making the kittens sneeze – and unpacked dishes and pans into their own kitchen dresser, which looked like something from a dolls' house in Finmory's kitchen.

Mr. Manders and Mike fixed up beds. "Not permanent, only somewhere to be going on with." Mrs. Manders tackled a bathroom and the room with the bay window that looked over the garden to the sea.

"Stop. Everybody out," boomed Mr. Manders, just when Petra and Jinny were beginning to think that he had forgotten about knocking off at four.

"Not until I have a cup of tea," said Mrs. Manders, pushing her hair out of her eyes and leaving streaks of grime over her forehead. "What a place. We'll all die of some dreaded dirt disease."

"Our lungs choked with dust like vacuum cleaner bags," agreed Jinny. "We'll need to empty them out."

They walked together down to the sea. On one side, the hills dropped steeply to the path, and on the other were two fields belonging to Mr. MacKenzie. To reach the beach, they had to climb a rampart of sea-smooth boulders, then slither and slide down an avalanche of pebbles to the small sandy bay, enclosed on both sides by pincer jaws of black, jagged rock. The sea pounded up the beach in thunderous, foam-crested breakers, and the air was loud with screaming gulls.

"Pinch me," commanded Jinny. "Wake me up. I'm dreaming."

Mike obliged and pinched her hard.

"Pig!" she screamed, and chased him madly over the sands until they fell in a struggling heap.

"Behave yourselves," said Petra. "What will people think?"

But there were no people, only the domed head of a seal watching them curiously from the safety of the water.

Jinny lay flat on her back staring up at the gulls as they soared and swung in mazy patterns with effortless sweeps of their powerful wings. And suddenly she was back in the circus ring. The memory of the chestnut horse drowned her in a wave of blackness. Where was the horse now? What right had she to be here with so much freedom and space, when the chestnut was probably standing in a dark horse-box, waiting for the evening performance when she would again be goaded into attacking the ringmaster.

Jinny sprang to her feet.

"I'm going back to the house," she shouted to the others, who were exploring rock pools.

"What's wrong?" she heard her mother call – and her father's voice telling them to leave her alone.

Jinny's feet slapped down on the uneven ground as she ran faster and faster, stumbling and tripping, the wind drying her tears. If she could only run hard enough and fast enough she would escape from the crack of the ringmaster's whip and the fear-filled eyes of the Arab.

Reaching their garden, Jimmy slowed down, rubbed her arm across her eyes and walked towards the house. In sight of the heavy front door, she stopped and stared. There was someone sitting on the step. A thin young man, his bent knees sharp under his faded jeans, his black sweater hanging loosely about him, his strawy hair long on his shoulders. He seemed to be asleep, with his head resting on his folded arms. At his side was a bulging pack and a shaggy mongrel held by a length of rope. The dog saw Jinny, pricked his ears and barked. The young man woke and looked up.

It couldn't possibly be. But it was.

"Ken!" Jinny yelled, "Ken!" and went full tilt, tearing up the path towards him.

"How you doin' then?" Ken asked, as he uncoiled himself from the step and stood up slowly, laughing at Jinny's delight.

"How did you find us?" Jinny demanded. "How did you know we were here?"

"Dropped in," said Ken. "Thought you might be needing a hand with the garden. Could do a little digging. Heard Tom was a potter now. Could give him a hand with that, too. Know a bit about it."

"You mean you're going to stay?"

"If you'll have me."

Jinny flung her arms wide, shook the weight of her long hair for brimming happiness.

"Of course we'll have you," she exclaimed.

Ken smiled down at her from his lanky height, his green eyes laughing with her. Jinny could never remember what Ken's face looked like. It was always changing. Other people wore masks that you could remember, but Ken's face was different.

"And this is Kelly," Ken said, indicating the dog. "He

25

came along. I was hitching a lift and he appeared beside me. Got into the cab with me and now he's here."

Kelly's yellow eyes looked straight at Jinny. Under his thatch of grey and brown hair he considered her distantly.

"Of course you can both stay," said Jinny. "You know you can."

Even Petra was pleased to see Ken.

"Exactly what we're needing," welcomed Mr. Manders. "A bit of brawn to help us reclaim this wilderness. Do your folks know you're here?"

For a second, the light went out of Ken's face. His eyes hardened to a cold watchfulness.

Mr. Manders waited. "I've got to ask. You know that, Ken. You're not eighteen yet."

Ken had been put on probation for breaking into a warehouse with four other boys. He had said nothing to defend himself, but on the last day of his probation he had said to Mr. Manders, "I'd nothing to do with it." "I never thought you had," Mr. Manders had replied.

"Seventeen this time round," said Ken. "I was over ninety not so long ago, but I don't expect you to consider that. Yes, my parents know. You can phone them to check up. They're even going to send me a cheque every month, they're so pleased to be rid of me."

What could it be like, Jinny thought, terrified, to belong to a family who didn't want you. She knew Ken's family weren't like most of the people her father had worked with. They were rich. A detached bungalow, a low slung car and a country cottage.

"Well, we want you," Jinny said loudly.

"I'll phone tomorrow," said Mr. Manders.

"Settled?" said Ken. "O.K.? I can unload, then." He opened his pack, laid a sleeping bag on the floor, and set out bags of brown rice, wholemeal flour and soya flour on the kitchen table. "Arranged with the shop in Stopton to send regular supplies, so I'll not cost much to keep."

"Come and see my mural," Jinny said, remembering it as they finished washing up the supper dishes.

Her father, Mike and Ken went with her. In the grey evening light, the red horse seemed to glow in the dark room.

26

"Wonder who painted it," said Mike, while Ken crouched down on his heels, examining it in silence.

"We went to a circus last night," began Jinny, "and there was a chestnut Arab . . ."

"Oh no," Mike groaned, "not again." And he and Mr. Manders went back downstairs while Ken stayed, silently listening to Jinny's heartbreak.

"And I can't do anything about her," Jinny said at last, reaching the end of her story.

"You shouldn't have gone," Ken said, his voice harsh. "Have nothing to do with people who put anything in cages."

"But that's zoos."

"Don't give it us," said Ken. "You know quite well what I'm saying."

He stretched upright, balancing on his toes, his eyes still on the painting of the red horse.

"But what can I do?" cried Jinny. "What can I do to save her?"

"We don't know what we can do," Ken told her. "We none of us know. You didn't know I'd be here tonight did you? Yet here I am."

He turned on silent, cat feet and left Jinny alone.

Not knowing why, Jinny went to find a sheet of paper and the box of pastels. Kneeling on the floor under the watching eyes of the red horse, Jinny drew a picture of the chestnut mare. Not as she had been at the circus, but galloping free over the Finmory hills, her mane and tail fanned out by the sea wind, her whole body alert and vivid with the smells, sights and sounds of the wild country.

When it was finished, Jinny stood looking down on the picture as if it had been drawn by someone else, or as if she had looked through the window to discover the horse galloping there.

Jinny stood for a long time just looking, and then she found a roll of sellotape and stuck the drawing of the Arab on the wall opposite the red horse.

CHAPTER FOUR

On their fourth morning at Finmory, Jinny woke early. For a second, she couldn't think where she was. The window was in the wrong place and her bed should have been the other way round. Then she remembered. Finmory!

Jinny jumped out of bed, and, picking her way through the assault course of books, boxes and clothes that covered her bedroom floor, she ran to the window. Beyond the tangled garden was the quicksilver line of the sea. Gulls soared above the stillness and the sky was blue and distant, without a cloud. It was going to be a blue day. Jinny felt it shiver through her. Too special a day for them all to go on scrubbing and disinfecting and arranging furniture. If they were going to spend their time slaving away in the house, they might as well have stayed in Stopton. No one, absolutely no one, not even her family, and certainly not Ken, could possibly want to work on a day like this, Jinny thought.

She went under the archway and looked out of her other window. The sun was still a luminous disc, neat as a new two-pence piece. The early morning light made the moors and hills more mysterious than usual. In the dark valleys of shadow anything might be lurking.

"That's where we'll go," Jinny said aloud to the red horse. "We'll go to the very top of the hills, so that we can see right down the other side. If you were real, we would go together."

Jinny stood staring resolutely at the red horse, but it was too late. She didn't want to ride over the mountains on the painted horse who could never be real, but on the chestnut Arab.

"It's no use. I've thought about her," Jinny admitted to herself as she turned round to face her drawing of the Arab. Where was she now? Still at Inverburgh, or already miles away? "I'll never see her again," murmured Jinny. "Never."

Other people were always telling her not to go on wanting things that she could never have. Forget about them, they told her. But how could she forget when she hadn't forgotten? She could only pretend she'd forgotten, and that was no use.

By breakfast time, the blue day had established itself – golden and green and blue. Even Mrs. Manders, who was keenest on carpets and curtains and washed windows, couldn't ignore the weather.

"Stay shut up in the house today, and, when you die, God will demand to know what you did with His great glorious gift. And you will say, 'I scrubbed my floors'," teased Mr. Manders. " 'Godliness is before cleanliness', He will roar, and down you will go to hell."

"No way," said Ken. "He will explain and give you another day to enjoy."

"Never mind that rubbish," said Petra. "Where shall we go? I think we should take a picnic down to the beach and sunbathe."

"Oh no!" exclaimed Jinny. "We're going up the mountains. To the very top. I knew when I woke up that that was what we'd all do today."

"Is that a fact?" said Petra.

"We'd be able to see for miles," said Mike.

"Oh yes," said Jinny. "I know. Come on."

Ken carried the haversack with sandwiches, flasks, fruit and lemonade.

"Let me know when it gets too heavy and I'll take a turn," said Mr. Manders.

"It won't," said Ken. "I let it carry itself."

They climbed over the rocky ground behind the house, stopping to push open the creaking door of the croft and peer into the cobwebbed, dust-filled space.

"My studio and pottery," said Mr. Manders.

"You'll have spiders' footprints all over your pots," said Mike. "And mice. They'll probably nibble the edges."

Mr. Manders trod warily over the rotting floorboards and turned on a tap at the sink. Pipes groaned and creaked, and thick peat-brown water burst out of the tap, choked to nothing, then spluttered out again.

"For goodness' sake turn it off, Tom," shouted Mrs.

29

Manders above the noise. "The whole building is going to fall down on top of you."

Mr. Manders turned off the tap and the shuddering stopped. He looked around at the decay and damp. "You are completely mad," he told himself. "You should be pulling this ruin down, not kidding yourself that it will ever be a pottery." For a moment he remembered his office in Stopton, with its modern furniture and fitted carpets.

"Very nice," said Ken's voice behind him. "Very nice indeed. We'll get it together in no time."

Mr. Manders jumped, not realising that Ken had come into the croft. The boy was looking around him, his eyes bright with enthusiasm.

"When I think of the times I've sat in that ticky-tacky bungalow bedroom, thinking of all I could do if I only had a place like this . . ."

"And now you've got it," said Mr. Manders.

Ken looked straight at Mr. Manders. "Thanks," he said.

Outside, Jinny turned cartwheels of impatience, entangling herself with Kelly, who had come up to inspect this unusual human behaviour.

They climbed over the rusty wire that separated the grounds of Finmory from the moors.

"There's a path," pointed Mike.

"Sheep track," said his father.

Jinny ran ahead of her family, sitting on boulders to watch as they came towards her, then running on ahead again. As she climbed upwards, the world unrolled beneath her. Every time she stopped to look back, new headlands, black as jet against the aquamarine sea, had sprung into sight. As she struggled up over each peak of hillside, moorland sprang up around her – marsh and rock, glimmering lochans, the calm reaches of Loch Varrich, and oceans of bracken rolled away from her. Finmory House and Mr. MacKenzie's farm were tiny Monopoly pieces set in the pattern of cultivated fields.

The hill grew steeper, and sometimes Jinny had to climb on hands and knees. Below her, her family stopped to examine Petra's heel. "A blister," Jinny thought, knowing from a lifetime's experience the tender state of her sister's feet. "They can't be going to stop now. Not when we're almost at the top. Well, I'm going on," she decided, and began the final scramble.

It took Jinny another ten minutes to reach the crest of the hill.

"Keep going. Don't give up," she muttered to herself, and then, with a final effort, she made it. She stood up to see the land stretching down on the other side in one, green, rolling sweep, to the grey, snail-trail of the road from Inverburgh. Cars and lorries were matchbox models. Jinny stood waving her arms and shouting for joy.

" 'Behold a giant am I'," she yelled, filled with the exhilaration of standing on top of the world.

Ken was the first to reach her. He stood beside her, laughing.

"Can they see us from their cars?" Jinny asked him.

"They wouldn't think to look," said Ken, swinging the haversack from his shoulders.

"I'm going to make a kite," said Mike, joining them, "and bring it up here to fly."

"Great," agreed Ken.

"What are those animals down there?" Jinny asked suddenly. "They're not cows, are they?"

"Well, they're not sheep," said Mike, looking at the seven or eight shapes that were grazing half-way down the hillside.

"Elephants?" suggested Ken. "Unicorns?"

Jinny stared, shading her eyes against the sun. They couldn't possibly be . . . But they were!

"Ponies," she screamed. "They're ponies!"

"Trust Jinny," said Mr. Manders, as the others reached the top of the hill. "Take her anywhere and all she finds is horses."

"I'm going down to see them," called Jinny, already running towards the ponies.

Her feet went faster and faster over the rough sloping ground. Ponies on the Finmory hills!

She ran full tilt until she was close to the little herd and then fell into a clump of heather to stop herself.

The ponies had seen her coming, and were standing watching her suspiciously, ears pricked through overgrown forelocks, forefeet planted primly together, ready to

31

whirl and gallop away from the intruder in an instant.

"It's all right," Jinny reassured them. "There's the good ponies. Steady now."

There were eight Shetland mares and five woolly-coated foals. Jinny plucked a handful of grass and held it out to a skewbald. The mare snorted warily, taking care to keep herself between Jinny and her foal.

"It doesn't look very special grass," Jinny agreed, "but I'll scratch you behind the ears and you'll like that. Bet you're itchy as anything under all that mane. I know what it's like having long hair in the summer."

As she spoke, Jinny eased herself closer to the Shetlands. Reluctantly, she supposed that she was too heavy to ride them, but maybe she could train one of them to pull a cart. Jinny was driving two of the ponies along the road to Inverburgh when her foot slipped on a tussock of reeds – she lost her balance and fell sprawling to the ground. She sat up to see rumps and tails vanishing over the hillside.

A man's voice laughed. Jinny jumped to her feet, and saw Mr. MacKenzie sitting on a boulder, grinning at her.

"Aye," he remarked, as if they were meeting in Inverburgh High Street, "it's a grand day."

"I never saw you. Were you there all the time?"

"Up taking a look over the ponies. Now and again I take a bit walk to myself and see how they're doing. On a fine day, you understand."

"Are they yours?"

"Aye."

"I was going to speak to them."

"I saw that. I was just about to stop you. That skewbald's a right bad one. Kick your head off as soon as look at you."

"Oh, she wouldn't. Not my head."

"As wild as tinks, the whole bunch of them."

"But doesn't anyone ride them?" demanded Jinny.

"Ride them?" Mr. Mackenzie spat derisively out of the corner of his mouth. "They haven't had a rope on them since they were foaled. I keep them for breeding, that's the thing for the cash these days. Off to America with them."

"Oh," said Jinny. She stared down at the road, watching

32

traffic that had grown into recognisable cars and lorries now that she was further down the hill. "I wasn't actually so much thinking of riding them," she admitted to the farmer. "More driving them?"

"Then think again, lass," suggested Mr. Mackenzie.

"Oh," said Jinny, wondering if he would really notice if one of his mares was missing, since he didn't seem to have much interest in them as individuals.

"And how's the family? Getting settled in?"

"We're up on the hill having a picnic . . ." began Jinny, her eyes still on the road, her mind half on the thought of a foal tied to the back of the cart as they trotted into Inverburgh. She saw four gaudily painted vans and trailers appear round the corner of the road from Inverburgh and thought, "What's that?" Then she thought, "Circus" and "Arab" at the same time, and felt the sun go out, the grey earth cold and made of metal. On the road beneath her, the chestnut Arab, shut in one of the horse-boxes, was being driven away from her for ever.

"Look at that stupid idiot," said Mr. MacKenzie, pointing with the stem of his pipe in the opposite direction from the circus vans.

Jinny saw a bright yellow oil tanker booming down the road, straight towards the circus vans.

"No bloomin' wonder folk are killed on that road."

The driver of the tanker could not see round the corner to the lumbering circus vans and the swaying sideshows stacked on the trailers. The driver of the first circus van could not see the bulk of the oil tanker speeding towards him. Only Jinny and Mr. MacKenzie could see the road on both sides of the blind corner.

The oil tanker was in the centre of the road as it took the bend.

"He'll hit them!" Jinny cried, her voice a helpless scream, for there was nothing she could possibly do to stop the accident happening.

Her nails dug into the ground as the oil tanker rounded the corner in the middle of the road, saw the circus vans, and swerved violently.

Jinny let out her breath. He had missed them. They were safe. The terrifying picture of the Arab's horse-box,

33

crushed into shattered wood – and screaming, wounded horses – vivid as colour telly, began to flicker out. Then the tanker's rear wheels seemed to skid, and the yellow, uncontrolled bulk swung across the road and rammed into one of the circus vans.

The sound of grinding metal reached them a fraction after they saw it happen, but already Jinny was tearing madly down the hillside.

"No place for a lass," shouted Mr. MacKenzie as he caught up with her. "May be people hurt. Get back with you."

Jinny hardly glanced at him. What did people matter when the Arab might need her? She could feel her lungs as pain in her back, the muscles in her legs burning, and her heart trying to jump through her throat, but she kept on running.

The driver of the oil tanker was slumped over the wheel. Men were struggling to open the truck door.

"The horses? Where are the horses?" shouted Jinny, but none of the circus people seemed to hear her. The van that had been hit was lying on its side with the trailer that it had been pulling concertina'd into it. From inside the trailer, Jinny could hear the crash of hooves and the screaming whinnying of terrified horses. Three men, one of whom Jinny recognised as the ringmaster, were trying to open the ramp at the back of the trailer.

"Here it comes, Joe," one of them yelled, as the ramp yawned open.

"Be ready to catch them in case they're loose," the ringmaster warned.

"Is the Arab in there?" Jinny demanded, but again no one seemed to hear her.

When the ramp was down, they led out the two rosinbacks – one with a bleeding gash on its shoulder.

"Get out of the way," the ringmaster swore at Jinny as she pushed past him, trying to see into the box. He swung his arm at her and she dodged back out of his reach, but she had had enough time to see that the horse still in the box was the Arab.

"Look out for this brute," the ringmaster shouted, as one of his men went into the box to move the parti-

34

tion that had separated the Arab from the other two horses.

Jinny craned forward to watch the man unhook the slatted barrier. She caught a glimpse of the Arab's head – sweated dark with fear, a frenzied eye rolling in a white socket, and ears clipped back – before the horse reared up, knocking the man aside, and came plunging desperately out of the box and down the ramp. From the end of the rope halter swung the metal bar to which the horse had been tied.

"She'll break her leg if she gets it caught in that," Jinny yelled. "Catch her. You've got to catch her."

For a split second the Arab stood, dazzled by the light, then reared again. The ringmaster snatched at the halter rope but dodged aside to miss the swinging metal bar.

Jinny saw the man miss the rope and the other people jump out of the way.

"Her legs," Jinny thought – and where the others jumped away, she threw herself against the Arab's shoulder, smelling the acid stench of the horse against her face, as her hands gripped the cheek pieces of the halter and dragged it down over the Arab's ears. The horse swerved and bucked, tossing her head violently. Jinny lost her balance and fell, but her hands were still knotted around the halter. The Arab was free.

With a piercing neigh, the horse surged up the hillside, rearing and bucking, standing for a moment of stillness like a heraldic beast, her head high and tail plumed. She screamed from the pits of her nostrils – and far up the hillside one of the Shetlands whickered shrilly in reply. The Arab gave one last tremendous buck, her hind hooves high in the air, crashing the gold cymbal of the sun, and then she was away – thundering, drumming – her galloping hooves beating their tattoo of freedom as she raced over the hillside.

Tears poured down Jinny's face, her whole body shook with sobbing. Behind her, the ringmaster swore in useless anger, and a police car swung in to the scene of the accident.

The policemen forced open the cab door and, twenty minutes later, the driver was on his way to hospital. The crashed vehicles had been pushed off the road and the two rosinbacks loaded into another trailer.

"You'll not get near your horse," Mr. MacKenzie told the ringmaster. "I'd need to round the Shetlands up and bring them all down to the farm. And I'll not be thinking of that for a month or two yet."

The ringmaster glared at the empty hillside. Jinny thought he was like a brimstone, pantomime devil.

"If I'd a gun, I'd shoot the useless brute," he muttered. "No saying when we'll be back this way again."

"I'll charge you a pound a week for grazing, or I'll give you twenty pounds for her," offered Mr. MacKenzie.

"Forty," said the ringmaster.

"Thirty," said Mr. MacKenzie, as he turned to walk away.

The ringmaster had to call him back to accept his offer. The farmer put his hand in his hip pocket, brought out a wad of dirty paper, and peeled off three ten-pound notes.

"Lucky for you Murdo took away the scrap this morning. I'll have a receipt, if you don't mind."

In the early evening, the Manders and Ken made their way back to Finmory. Jinny walked silently beside her father.

"I don't know how you manage it," he said.

"Neither do I," said Jinny.

"You're not bounding very much," said Petra nastily, because her blister was hurting and she needed a quarrel to take her mind off it. "Usually, when something like this happens to you, you're all over the place."

"Not this," said Jinny, patiently explaining. "You don't bound when the most wonderful thing in the world has just happened to you. You feel empty somehow."

And she walked on, seeing the stone walls of Finmory, the hills sleeked smooth after the day's sun and the far, mirror glint of the sea. Yet, more clearly than any of these, Jinny saw the reaching neck of the Arab, her winnowing fringe of mane and her ears alive to the sound of her rider's voice as Jinny rode her home to Finmory.

CHAPTER FIVE

It was a week before Jinny even glimpsed the Arab again.

"They smell me coming," she declared.

"I'm not surprised," said Petra.

"You're meant to keep down below the skyline," advised Mike.

Jinny tried crawling through the bracken, and her arms came out in a rash.

"I think I'm allergic to bracken," she sighed, " – and it was working. I got quite close to them."

"How close?" asked Petra.

"Well . . ."

"Close enough to see them without a telescope?"

"Sort of," admitted Jinny.

Ken went with her, one afternoon, to see if he could help.

"The problem," said Jinny, "is that they've got miles and miles and miles of moorland to graze over, and the Shetlands know it and I don't. There I am, crawling along, all flies and itch, while they are standing on the next hilltop, laughing at me. And even when I do see them, they gallop off and I can't find them again."

"Difficult," agreed Ken.

"She's the worst," said Jinny. "Standing there like a giraffe, ready to warn the Shetlands if a bird as much as moves on the horizon."

"We won't find them if you can't stop talking," said Ken.

"I'm usually by myself," said Jinny indignantly, "so it can't be that." But she stopped talking, and followed in Ken's silent footsteps.

After about two hours' tracking, they caught a glimpse of the ponies grazing on the shoulder of the next hill. Most of the mares had their heads down, stuffing themselves industriously, while their foals were paper cut-outs pasted in the pools of shadow beneath rocky outcrops. Only the

Arab standing apart, snatching a mouthful of grass, then looking warily about her while she ate it.

Ken had hardly put his finger to his lips to tell Jinny that the horses were in sight, when the Arab's warning neigh bannered the silence. Hardly pausing to check, the mares wheeled and were away. The foals bumbled into sudden life and cantered, stiff-legged, at their mothers' sides. At their head the Arab floated, swift as a bright, wind-blown cloud shadow.

Jinny held her breath as she watched them gallop out of sight. For a split, pico second the air was disturbed by their furious stampede and then it settled again into stillness.

"She is beautiful," murmured Jinny longingly, her breath escaping with the words, as she flung herself down on the ground. "And you needn't think that if we go on we'll find them on the other side of the hill because we won't. They just vanish. Today's been a good day. At least we've seen her."

" True," said Ken.

"But that's no use," exclaimed Jinny, springing to her feet – spreading her hands wide to emphasize her words. "It's no use. How am I ever going to ride her when I can't get near her?"

"She doesn't intend to let you. And I don't blame her. If I'd escaped from a circus you wouldn't get near me, either. Give her time."

"But she's got to get to know me," said Jinny despairingly.

"You'll never get near her this way," said Ken. "Discover a place they're fond of, where they go a lot. To them, this moor's like Stopton was to us. Places where you go when it's hot; places for night time, best place to be in the early morning. It doesn't look to them the way it does to us. Find one of their favourite places and hide there until they come."

Jinny nodded. It was the best suggestion anyone had made yet.

"And call her Shantih."

"What?" said Jinny.

"You haven't found a name for her, have you?"

38

"No," Jinny admitted. "She was Yasmin in that circus; but I'm not calling her that."

"Then call her Shantih. It means peace. Makes a difference what you call people. Names alter things."

Jinny didn't see that they did, but she liked the sound of the word. "Shan-tih," she said slowly. "O.K. Shantih. That's her name."

But being rechristened Shantih instead of Yasmin didn't seem to have much effect on the Arab. She still fled like a red-gold ghost whenever she sensed Jinny's presence. Jinny tried picking one place and waiting there, hopefully hidden in the bracken, but Shantih seemed to know where she was and kept the Shetlands well away from her.

"Sometimes I despair," Jinny moaned to her sister a fortnight later.

"Sometimes we despair," Petra said, "of you ever helping us to get this house in order."

"My rooms are done," said Jinny, feeling slightly guilty.

"Your rooms!" said Petra. "Now that is really decent of you. Really big of you to go to all the trouble of taking your clothes out of your case and putting them into your wardrobe."

"I've done more than that," said Jinny. "I've pinned my posters on the wall and . . ." She paused, trying desperately to think of something else that would equal the kitchen garden Ken had started; the seemingly endless scrubbing, cleaning and decorating that everyone except herself had been doing, and her father's and Ken's transformation of the broken-down croft into a reasonable pottery. She couldn't think of anything. Glancing at Petra, Jinny didn't feel that her sister would be impressed by her drawings of spiders, beetles and flies that Jinny had made while she lay hidden, waiting for a glimpse of Shantih. Jinny herself thought they were quite good. She thought about them now to take her mind off Petra's expectant, smug face. She had made herself really look at the insects so that they stopped being "Yeugh" creepies and became fascinating creations, a whole underbracken world that had nothing to do with the giant crash of humans.

"See," exclaimed Petra triumphantly, "you can't think of one other thing you've done to help."

"Well, you can't say I've been lying in bed," Jinny protested.

"Next best thing," said Petra.

Jinny decided to retire gracefully. She went to look for her mother. In the Stopton flat you had always known where people were by just listening, but at Finmory you had to safari round before you found anyone. Jinny stopped at the kitchen to stock up with biscuits, in case she should miss her mother the first time round and have to circle the house twice. Glancing back at the trail of biscuit crumbs, Jinny wondered if it might be possible to lure Shantih with a trail of oats, but she decided that the sheep would probably eat them, and went on looking until she found her mother painting a bathroom.

"Can I help you?" she asked.

Mrs. Manders looked at her doubtfully. "Don't get it in your hair," she warned, handing Jinny a brush.

"'Course not," said Jinny, sloshing the brush into the white emulsion and attacking what seemed a suitable wall. "I'm helping because Petra says I haven't."

"True," agreed her mother. "But it's all right. I'd rather see you outside. Won't be long until you're back at school."

"Oh, weeks yet," said Jinny.

"Not here. Scottish schools start at the beginning of September. You start next Thursday, and Petra goes off the day before. It will be strange not having her at home all the time."

"No!" Jinny cried, swinging the brush in the air and cascading herself and her mother with paint.

"Look at the mess, Jinny. Do be careful."

"I thought we'd weeks yet. Weeks and weeks. I'll never catch Shantih before next Thursday. Never."

"The horse won't vanish because you go to school."

"But don't you see," cried Jinny, waving her brush wildly in the air, "I've got to be able to ride her before I go to school."

"Stop waving that brush around. You'll have the place covered in paint."

"I must be able to ride her before we go to school, because you're going to buy us ponies to ride to school and it MUST be Shantih for me."

40

"So this is what you've been imagining. But there's not a chance. We are going to get you a pony, but never Shantih. Even if she were half tame, she wouldn't be suitable."

"She would," said Jinny, scrubbing paint into the wall. "Oh, yes she would."

When Mr. Manders heard Jinny's idea, he only said, "Bring her down to the house and I'll have a look at her."

"You know I can't get near her," said Jinny, spacing every word slowly and deliberately.

"Yes, I know," said Mr. Manders, "and that's why we're going to see Miss Tuke tomorrow. She runs a pony trekking centre, and she's agreed to let us have two of her trekking ponies until next June."

Jinny went to bed still black and sulky.

"You're being silly, Jinny Manders," she told herself severely. "Tomorrow you're going to get a pony and that's what you've always wanted, isn't it? So what?" replied the bit of Jinny that always seemed more real than all the common sense in the world. "So what? That's not what I want now." And Jinny pulled the bedclothes over her head, screwed up her eyes and curled herself up into a tight, defiant knot.

Mr. Manders, Mike and Jinny drove to the trekking centre the next afternoon. Miss Tuke was pleased to see them.

"I can't tell you how glad I am when someone reliable offers to take over any of my ponies for the winter. That's where my profits go. And I'm sure I can trust you. I've heard all about you from Mrs. MacKenzie. So nice for them having a family at Finmory again, especially after that last lot. Utterly impossible, they were. Now, have you ridden a little?"

Jinny said she had. Mike said he hadn't but he felt as if he knew how to, like knowing how to swim even before you could.

"Good show," said Miss Tuke without conviction. "You'd better have Punch, then. He's certain he knows how to look after humans. And Bramble for you, my dear."

Jinny scowled up at her, still trying to pretend that she wasn't feeling excited.

"Really it's an Arab I want, not a Highland," she informed Miss Tuke.

"But how unsuitable," stated Miss Tuke, and led them down to a paddock where two Highland ponies were standing nose to tail, keeping the flies off each other.

Miss Tuke gave the children a halter each. "Punch is the grey and Bramble the black. Now let me see you catch them."

Jinny dragged the halter rope behind her and walked slowly up to the black pony, who was dozing peacefully. She slipped the rope over his neck, and the pony opened his eyes and regarded Jinny with a cynical gaze. He pushed at her anorak pocket, nudging hopefully, and, despite all her determination, Jinny's mouth stretched into a grin. She fitted the halter on to the pony's head, pulling his furry ears through the head piece and straightening his bushy forelock, then she clapped his thick-set neck, already woolly with his winter coat. He was to be her pony. Not Shantih, but, all the same, her pony.

She led him back to the gate, where Miss Tuke was telling their father about feeding and shoeing. "Hay and pony nuts," she was saying. "As long as they have adequate shelter, they're better outside."

"Well done, dear," she said to Jinny and went to help Mike, who was in danger of hobbling Punch with the halter.

Under Miss Tuke's watchful eye, they took a dandy brush over the ponies and saddled them up.

"Now we'll see how you get on with them," Miss Tuke said, as Jinny and Mike struggled on to the ponies' backs.

"Trek forward," shouted Miss Tuke in a loud voice, and the ponies moved sedately forward in first gear. "If they're ever having you on, remember those magic words – 'Trek forward'. Never fails. Now take them down to the paddock and ride them round."

Even when she was falling off them, Jinny had always thought that the ponies at the Stopton Riding School were on the slow side, but compared to Bramble and Punch they had been atomic. Obeying Miss Tuke's instructions, they walked the ponies round, halted them, mounted and dismounted, and walked them round again.

Jinny glanced back at Mike. He was sitting comfortably astride the Highland, looking completely at ease. "Trust Mike," Jinny thought. Riding was going to be another of the things that Mike did naturally and couldn't care less about. Jinny groaned, and turned back to concentrate on keeping her heels down, her knees against the saddle and her legs in what she hoped was the correct position.

"Try a trot," suggested Miss Tuke.

Jinny shortened her reins and applied the correct aids as taught by Major Young's assistant. Bramble plodded on, head down. Jinny pressed her legs tighter against the hairy bulk of horse.

"Trot," she said. "Trot on." Bramble flicked an ear.

"You'll need to wake him up," said Miss Tuke. "Kick him on. They don't do much trotting out on the treks, but once you have them to yourselves they'll soon start to put a little more effort into life. Now Bramble, move. Get on with you."

Encouraged by Miss Tuke, Jinny kicked hard. She felt Bramble's plod turn into a walk.

"That's the way," encouraged Miss Tuke, and Jinny kicked harder, stirrups and heels banging the pony's sides.

"There, you've done it. He's away," cheered Miss Tuke.

For a second, Jinny felt the pony change into a trot. She banged her heels hard into his sides. Bramble stopped dead, twitched his quarters in a token buck and Jinny went flying into the air. Before she had time to realise what had happened she was sitting on the ground, while Bramble looked down at her, ears pricked, nostrils wiffling, an expression of innocent amazement on his face.

Jinny sprang to her feet, fumbled the reins over the pony's neck and clambered back into the saddle.

"Now," she told the pony, "you needn't think you're getting away with that. I'm in charge here and when I say trot, we trot." As she spoke, Jinny urged Bramble forward, her elbows flapping, heels kicking and her seat bumping up and down in the saddle as she forced Bramble to trot. "Get on with you. Get on."

Bramble tried another half-hearted buck, but this time

43

Jinny was ready for him. She pulled up his head and sent him on.

"He'll canter for you," shouted Miss Tuke.

Jinny sat down and Bramble was cantering. She felt as if she was going faster than a Derby winner. Sky and hills, Miss Tuke and her father were blurred with speed. The clasp fell out of Jinny's hair, which streamed out behind her as they cantered round. She forgot everything except the hairy pony and this new-found delight of speed.

"Enough," called Miss Tuke. "Slow down."

Jinny heard her as if she were hailing them from outer space. She wanted to go on forever, never to stop.

"That'll do, Jinny," called her father's voice, and reluctantly Jinny steadied Bramble to a trot, then to a walk. She clapped the pony's neck and shoulder. "Bet you enjoyed that as much as I did," she whispered.

"That was super," said Mike, and for the first time since she had been bucked off Jinny remembered her brother.

"Were you cantering?" she asked him. "Are you O.K.?"

"'Course I'm O.K. Punch did the cantering. I just sat here."

"Oh," said Jinny, realising as they rode back towards Miss Tuke that Mike had been able to trot and canter without any trouble. She snorted in disgust, remembering the painful hours she had spent in Major Young's paddock learning to post.

"Well, I can see you'll manage them," Miss Tuke said, laughing at Jinny. "Don't suppose he'll try it on again. If he does, just sort him out the way you did just now."

"Did I?" said Jinny.

"You did," said Miss Tuke.

They rode the ponies back to Finmory, Miss Tuke promising that she would be over before the end of the week to see that they were settling down.

The ride home was mainly plod – sometimes plod that gradually became standstill until Jinny and Mike roused the ponies with cries of "Trek forward".

When they reached home, they turned out Punch and Bramble into the field between their garden and the sea.

"I can watch them from my bedroom window," thought Jinny, as the ponies rolled luxuriantly, and her family made

44

aren't-they-hairy type remarks. But it wasn't only two shaggy Highlands that Jinny saw. Almost as clearly as if she had been there, Jinny could see Shantih, her chestnut coat dazzling in the setting sun, her lifted head and her dark liquid eyes drinking in the magic and wonder that humans could only dream about.

"But of course!" Jinny exclaimed aloud.

"What?" demanded Ken.

"Oh, nothing," said Jinny hurriedly, for no one must know, not even Ken, in case they tried to stop her. The idea was so obvious that Jinny couldn't understand why she hadn't thought of it before. She would ride Bramble over the moors to find the Shetlands, and when she found them, Shantih would think it was only another horse. She wouldn't be afraid. She wouldn't run away. "I'll go to-night," Jinny promised herself, and shivered, goose-over-her-grave, with excitement.

Jinny sat on her bedroom floor between the mural of the red horse and her own picture of Shantih. She was drawing Highland ponies, trying to capture the expression on Bramble's face when he had bucked her off; trying to draw the way they stood, resting a hind hoof, muzzles almost touching the ground as if they had been there without moving for centuries. She was drawing because it was the best way to fill in the waiting until her family were all in bed.

Her mother knocked on the door, telling Jinny to stop reading, put her light out and go to sleep. Jinny switched her light off and sat in the patch of white, moon-cold beams that streamed through the window. Cisterns gurgled and chugged, bedroom doors banged shut. Jinny listened to the silence – her ears creeping. She stared through the windows at the hills that shouldered dark against the moon-bright sky. Tiptoeing to the other window, she could see the huge globe of the moon – so low and heavy that Jinny could have touched it if she had wanted. The sea between the jet-black cliffs was luminous, quicksilver, and the two ponies were dark, rounded shapes against silvered grass.

Jinny swallowed dryly. She was afraid, afraid to go out alone into this bleak, two-dimensional world. There might

45

be anything out on the mountains on a night like this. Perhaps she should go tomorrow . . .

"Jinny Manders, you are a coward," she said under her breath, and stood on her head the way Ken had taught her to do. He said it calmed your nerves. Then she put on her anorak and made her way through the sleeping house, out into the moonlit garden.

She found Bramble's bridle in the outhouse that was to be the ponies' stable, and, wading through deep pools of shadow, she went down to the field. Bramble allowed himself to be caught without any trouble. Jinny squeezed him through the gate, only just managing to shut it before Punch got through as well. She sprang up on to Bramble and urged him forward.

The black pony, sensing Jinny's determination, walked out steadily, while Punch screamed his desertion, trotting madly up and down the hedge, lungeing against the gate. Jinny watched the house, dreading to see a light come on in one of the bedrooms. But the black gap windows remained dark, and Jinny rode on up the hillside.

She was fairly certain where the Shetlands and Shantih would be. She knew that in the evening they usually made their way to a ring of standing stones, and Jinny thought that they must spend the night there. She knew the way – first, a fairly clear track through the bracken, which took you to a burn; you followed the burn up over the hillside, and from there you could see the jagged shards of rock silhouetted against the skyline. That was where she would find Shantih.

Sure-footed and willing, Bramble picked his way over the rough ground. "I expect you're glad to get out on your own instead of being stuck in a line with all those others," Jinny chatted. The pony flickered his muffed ears to the sound of her voice.

It was bitterly cold. So cold that Jinny's feet in their sandshoes changed from cold to pain and then into nothing. Her legs stopped above her ankles. She buried her hands in Bramble's mane for warmth, and was glad she was riding bareback, feeling the living, comforting bulk of the pony as part of herself.

A bird screeched, ripping the silence, making the skin

46

tighten on Jinny's neck. The mountains seemed to shrug in closer as she rode, and the moon was a single eye staring straight down on her. "Shantih, Shantih, Shantih," Jinny whispered under her breath, using the name as a charm to control her imagination and stop it stampeding into werewolves and unstoned dead who wandered by night. Bramble's hooves clattered on loose stones, and crushed through bracken and heather as he walked steadily on.

When they left the stream to go up the hillside towards the standing stones, Bramble's pace quickened, his neck arched and he whickered softly. Jinny had to hold him back from breaking into a trot.

"Steady," she whispered. "Easy now. It's too rough to trot." But she felt her stomach turn over with the same excitement. She was right. The herd must be at the standing stones. Jinny crouched close to Bramble. She pressed her cheek against his neck, riding with her arms low.

They heard the Arab's challenging whinny, and then saw her – black against the skyline. She came towards them at a racking trot, circled them suspiciously, her tail high over her quarters, the moon shadows accentuating the dark pits of her eyes and nostrils and carven head. Bramble stood stock still, squealing when Shantih came too close. Jinny lay on Bramble's neck without a movement, only following Shantih with her eyes. The Arab came closer. She stretched out her neck, blowing over the strange pony. Jinny felt the warm breath on her hand. Bramble squealed, but didn't move. They stood poised, nostril to nostril, the thick-set, stolid black Highland and the Arab, all fleet and fire, flame frozen under the moon.

Jinny stretched out her arm and ran her hand down Shantih's sleek neck.

There was a moment when Jinny thought the Arab was going to stay; a moment when she was gentle under Jinny's caress. But it was only a moment, over before Jinny could allow herself to believe that it was happening. Then, with a wild whirl of mane and tail, a bunching, clattering panic, Shantih had charged through the watching Shetlands and they had all vanished into the night. Bramble plunged to

47

follow them, but Jinny managed to control him and turn him back to Finmory.

Ken and Kelly were at the field gate when Jinny got back.

"I reckoned that was where you'd be," said Ken, when Jinny told him. "I came out to shut this idiot up. Thought he'd wake your whole family and then there would have been trouble."

Ken held open the field gate, and Jinny rode Bramble through and returned him to Punch.

"How did it go?" asked Ken.

Jinny hung herself over the gate, waiting for her feet and legs to return to life.

"Did you get near her?"

"Yes," Jinny said. "Yes. I touched her. She let me touch her."

CHAPTER SIX

Jinny rang the schoolhouse bell and waited. She hadn't wanted to come, but her father had insisted that she and Mike should ride to Glenbost, introduce themselves to Mr. Gorman, the schoolmaster, and make sure that there was a field and shelter for the ponies while they were at school.

"Seeing it's the last day of the holidays only makes it all the more necessary," Mr. Manders had insisted impatiently, his mind on driving Petra to her school hostel that afternoon. "What are you going to do tomorrow if there isn't a field? Hold their reins through the classroom window?"

"There's nothing but fields," said Jinny, stating the obvious.

"You need a field with a fence round it," said Mr. Manders. "I agree with you there is nothing but grass, but wild grass is quite different to a tame field."

"Perhaps Mr. Gorman would like to see you before the term starts," suggested Mrs. Manders. "I know they did at Stopton."

"This is not Stopton," snapped Jinny. She had been

planning to have a last ride over the moors in the hope of seeing Shantih again, before the prison gates of education closed her in, leaving her only weekends of freedom. "I feel it in my bones that Jinny Manders and Glenbost School are not going to compatabalize."

"Wherever did you get that word from?" asked her father in disgust.

"Made it up," said Jinny, "or my bones did. They feel incompatabilization towards that school."

Before she rang the schoolhouse bell, Jinny had peered through the high classroom window. About eight, old fashioned, double desks were arranged in rows. In one corner of the room was a low table and four small chairs. There were two blackboards. On one were arithmetic problems about taps filling baths, trains arriving at stations and shopping bills. The other was covered with cramped handwriting that Jinny couldn't read, and the instruction to parse and analyse. The only touch of colour in the whole room was an ABC pinned on the wall beside the low table.

"Bones," thought Jinny, "as usual you were right." And she walked like a prisoner to the scaffold and rang the schoolhouse bell.

"Ring it again," shouted Mike, when no one came. Jinny gave the bell another ring and told Mike to stop letting the ponies eat the hedge.

She stood fidgeting on the doorstep. "Our last day," she thought, "and we're stuck here. Oh, come on, come on." And being pretty sure that there was no one in the schoolhouse, Jinny kept her finger hard down on the bell button.

A man's footsteps came clattering downstairs. Jinny hardly had time to take her finger off the bell before the door was thrown open. The tall man whom Jinny had glimpsed from their car on their first day at Finmory stood there. Mr. Gorman, Jinny presumed. He had obviously been asleep. The ruff of grey hair that fringed his bald, domed head was flattened on one side of his head and fluffy on the other, the neck of his shirt was open and his eyes had the shocked state of someone who has been woken up suddenly.

"Good afternoon," said Jinny, hoping that Mr. Gorman
49

would hear it as polite, which it was meant to be, and not cheeky, which she was afraid it sounded.

"Did you ring that bell, girl?" demanded Mr. Gorman.

"Yes," said Jinny. "I think my father arranged . . ."

"Never dare to come to this door again and ring my bell in that manner."

As Mr. Gorman shouted, his face became bright red. Jinny stared, fascinated, as the scarlet flush spread over his bald head and down below the neck of his shirt.

"Do I make myself clear?" Mr. Gorman's nose curved over his wet baby lips, his bullet eyes orbited their sockets like mad molecules. "Do I make myself quite clear?"

Jinny gulped.

"What do you want?"

"I want Shantih," thought Jinny. "I want nothing else in my whole life except to ride Shantih and paint pictures. That's what I want."

She stared up at Mr. Gorman, who was beginning to fade into a pink glow, and couldn't think what she was doing there.

"Don't stare at me with that insolent look on your face."

"The ponies," gasped Jinny. "Is there a field for them while we're at school?"

"So that's who you are. From Finmory, eh? Well, we've had the likes of you before. We've seen your type come and we've seen you go. But listen to this, my girl, while you're here you come to school every day. Do you understand?"

"Of course. We always do."

"Don't you dare answer me back," shouted Mr. Gorman, going scarlet again. "Now get off my doorstep and out of my garden. Pupils use the other gate."

"Sorry," said Jinny, and retreated to Mike.

"But didn't you ask about the field?" said Mike.

"Couldn't. He's mad."

They went into the shop and asked Mrs. Simpson. She came to the door and pointed out the field.

"Now, it'll be that wee field there, where you'll leave the beasties. The lot from Finmory used to leave their ponies there, that's when they bothered themselves to attend at all. A crowd of hippies if you ask me. With the
50

long hair and the beads and the beards. Chanting to some heathen idol. We were fair relieved to see the last of them."

Mike and Jinny checked the field fences and made sure there was water and shelter, then rode home.

"Long hair and beads and beards," imitated Mike. "What terrible people. We'll need to cover Dad and Ken up before we allow them out."

"We'll send Petra for all the shopping," giggled Jinny, but the thought of shopping had reminded her of the problems on the blackboard. Perhaps they hadn't been left over from last term. Perhaps they would be waiting for her tomorrow morning.

"It's taken us nearly an hour," said Mike. "We'd better leave before eight tomorrow morning, just to be sure we're not late on our first day."

Reluctantly, Jinny agreed. To hear Mike say before eight tomorrow filled her with the cold, hollowness of knowing that it was really going to happen.

But it was after half-past eight when they left Finmory the next morning. Mrs. Manders had felt that plaits would be more suitable for school. As usual, Jinny had disagreed, and it had taken them nearly a quarter of an hour to arrive at their usual compromise of tying Jinny's hair back. The ponies had been difficult to catch, and at the last minute Mrs. Manders had come running after them, waving Jinny's navy school skirt.

"I can't ride in a skirt."

"Take it with you. There's bound to be somewhere you can change. The teacher didn't sound to me as if he would welcome you in jeans."

"Well, give it to me," said Jinny crossly, and she stuffed the skirt into her schoolbag. "Now come on, or we're going to be late for lunch."

"It's all your fault," snapped Mike – so that Jinny knew he was feeling as uptight as she was. "I wouldn't have been late by myself."

"We'll gallop," commanded Jinny. "Kick them. Kick them hard."

But a trot was the most they managed. Speed in the morning was not acceptable to the trekking ponies' union.

"Aye, you two are for it," said Mr. Simpson, standing in his shop doorway. "Here, I'll see to them for you."

Gratefully, Jinny and Mike dismounted and gave their reins to Mr. Simpson.

"Are we very late?" asked Jinny.

"Half an hour. It'll be the belt for you both."

"What did he mean – the belt?" Mike asked, as they ran across the road to the school.

"Probably hang us from the ceiling with a belt," said Jinny. "He's crazy enough for anything."

They stopped in front of the school door to catch their breath.

"Look at our hands," said Mike.

Jinny looked. Her hands weren't just dirty, they were caked with mud and grease from Bramble. She gave them a useless rub on the seat of her jeans. "It's too late to do anything about them now," she said. "Come on. This is it." And she lifted the latch and pushed the door open.

Mr. Gorman was sitting at a high desk. The children, seated in rows, glanced up quickly then back down again. One of the smaller boys sitting at the low table was crying into his plasticine.

"Come in. Come right in. We're very pleased to have visitors. Aren't we?"

The class looked up again.

"Well, aren't we? Answer."

"Yes, sir," they answered with one voice, and having been given permission to play a part, they put down their pencils and stared at the strangers.

"We're sorry we're late," began Jinny, and to her dismay her voice came out high and shaky, "but . . ."

Mr. Gorman banged his clenched fist on the desk. He stood up, his black gown vulture-winged about him and the scarlet spread over his face.

"We don't have 'buts' in this school. We come to school on time."

"The ponies," squeaked Jinny.

"Ah yes, proper little Harvey Smiths, aren't you. Taxi's not good enough for you? I dare say your father will be one of these do-gooders, looking after the world that's done very well without him for the past million or so years. Is that right? Is that right?"

"Yes," said Jinny, "it is. That's why we're here. Dad didn't want to live in the city any longer. He says cities are destroying us, that we've got to find a simpler way to live. Move to the country and grow our own food . . ."

Mr. Gorman's thunderous silence made Jinny's voice fade away. Perhaps he didn't want an answer to his question.

"Is that so now? An environmentalist? Isn't that the word you'd use? Well, I'll tell you the word I use. The word all decent, hard-working people use."

Jinny stood mesmerised, staring up at Mr. Gorman, who seemed to have swollen into a scarlet-faced monster, beak-nosed, ready to swoop down on her.

"Layabouts, that's the word we use. Isn't it?" he demanded from his captive class.

"Yes, sir," their voices responded.

Jinny wanted to shout back at him, to shout the words she would use to describe *him*, but to her disgust she felt tears brimming in her eyes. She bit hard into her bottom lip to stop it trembling.

"Our father was a probation officer," said Mike clearly. "And if you think probation officers are layabouts, I don't think you know much about them."

For a second, Jinny thought Mr. Gorman was going to explode.

"Sit down," he roared. "Sit down."

Blindly, Jinny turned towards the rows of desks.

"There at the back, girl. Next to Dolina. And you, boy, there."

Jinny found herself sharing a double desk with a large, black-haired girl. Mr. Gorman threw an exercise book, a reading book, a spelling book and a pencil on to the desk and told Jinny to get on with the work on the blackboard. Surreptitiously, Jinny wiped her eyes and started on the only problem she knew how to do. When she had copied it out, she sat hunched over her desk, staring in silence at the pencilled numbers.

At lunchtime, Dolina showed her where they sat on the cloakroom pipes to eat their sandwiches.

"Do you think you'll be liking it here?" Dolina asked.

"No," said Jinny.

"Well, my mother says that it's a good grounding we get with Mr. Gorman. None of that nonsense but we can all read and write."

"I can read and write," said Jinny, "and we did lots of other things Music and Movement, and making things, and painting and poetry and plays."

Dolina turned pale cod eyes on Jinny's enthusiasm. "Och, we wouldn't be wasting our time with such rubbish."

"It wasn't rubbish. We did great things. We made a monster once, nearly as high as the ceiling, out of wire and papier maché. I painted the head and we gave her bicycle lamps for eyes, and we all went back one night to see her lit up in the dark."

Dolina stared into the middle distance.

"Why does your father make you ride those cart-horses?"

"Make us ride them?" Jinny echoed incredulously. "Having a pony to ride is one of the best things about Finmory."

"But you'll not have hot water?" Dolina demanded. "My mother says she wouldn't be living there, not for the pension."

In the afternoon, they sat with their reading books open on their desks, and one by one Mr. Gorman called them out to the front of the class to read.

"Where are you up to?" Jinny whispered to Dolina.

"Page 23," Dolina whispered back. "But you'll have to start at the beginning."

"Come out the child who spoke," roared Mr. Gorman.

Jinny started guiltily.

"Was it you, Jennifer Manders? Stand up. I'm talking to you. Did you speak?"

"Dolina was telling me," stuttered Jinny.

"So it was you, Dolina Thompson. The first day back and you can't keep your mouth shut. Well, it will be no change. Come out here."

Jinny's mouth opened and shut but she made no sound.

She wanted to say that she'd spoken first, that she'd only been asking Dolina about the reading.

"I was only . . ." Dolina began.

Mr. Gorman gripped her by the shoulder and dragged her close to his desk.

"Did you or did you not speak?"

"Yes," said Dolina.

"Then let's get it over with."

"It was me," Jinny tried again, but no one seemed to hear her protesting squeak.

Mr. Gorman took something out of his desk. He stood up in front of Dolina. "Hold out your hand," he said.

Dolina stood, stupidly holding out her hand, palm upwards. There was no sound in the room. All the children stared at Mr. Gorman and the fat lump of Dolina, standing there holding out her hand. Jinny watched as if it were television. She knew she was frightened, but she didn't know why. She tried again to tell Mr. Gorman that she had spoken first, but her throat was nightmare tight and she couldn't say anything.

The thing Mr. Gorman had taken from his desk unrolled into a strip of leather, two-tongued. He raised his arm, let the leather strap hang down his back and with his other hand he straightened out Dolina's fingers.

Suddenly the bubble burst and Jinny knew what was going to happen. This was the belt that Mr. Simpson had been talking about. Mr. Gorman was going to hit Dolina and she had to stand there and let him; and really it should have been herself, Jinny Manders, standing there. She stared in horror. In her whole life, Jinny had never seen a child punished like this.

"And it's all my fault," Jinny thought. "I spoke first. But I didn't know. Miss Dickson didn't mind us talking." Jinny saw for an instant the bright Stopton classroom – flowers and paintings, the Book Corner, the Music Corner and the Discovery Corner, the tea chest overflowing with old cloths for Drama, and the smell of the white mice.

The belt cut through the air and cracked into Dolina's hand. Jinny was sick before she could get out of the room.

"I'm never going back there," Jinny told Mike as they rode home. "Never."

Punch could only be persuaded to trek forward with his nose almost touching Bramble's rump. It made conversation difficult, but meant that Mike couldn't see that she was crying.

"You heard what they called me. 'Clipe'. It means telltale. But I didn't mean to. I tried to tell him it was my fault."

"Ian MacKenzie says he belts all the time. He says it doesn't hurt. They're all used to it. Dolina is always being belted for talking."

"I'm never going back."

"You've got to."

"I'd die if he tried to hit me. I'd fight him."

"You must go to school."

"Daddy won't let us go there when he knows what it's like."

"If you make enough fuss," warned Mike, "you'll have us back in Stopton."

"I don't care," said Jinny. "I'm not going near that man ever again."

"If you get back home tonight and start on, the way you can, you'll have us all back in Stopton. And I don't want that. I love it here."

"I don't care."

"But you care about Shantih. You can't expect another circus van to bring her down to Stopton and crash outside the front door."

Jinny didn't reply. She swallowed hard, scrubbed at her eyes with her knuckles and straightened her shoulders. If Mr. Gorman belted her every day, if she had to spend the next two years doing nothing but problems and parsing, she could never leave Finmory, not while Shantih was there.

"Come on, let's canter," Jinny shouted, and she startled Bramble into a sudden gallop.

CHAPTER SEVEN

By the end of October, Jinny's schooldays had settled into a pattern of numb endurance. None of the other children spoke to her. If she tried to speak to them, they shouted, "Tell tale tit, your tongue shall split, and all the little doggies shall have a little bit." So Jinny stopped trying to explain, and spent her lunchtimes with Bramble and Punch. She shared their lean-to shed if it was raining, and if it was dry she took Bramble for a ride, escaping for half an hour into a pretend world of being a hunted outlaw with a price on her head.

With a bit of help in the evenings from her mother, Jinny learnt how to do the arithmetic problems and the knack of parsing and analysis, which made up the day in Glenbost School. If Mr. Gorman was feeling pleased with himself, he allowed the children who had finished the set work on the blackboards to look at a volume of Chamber's Encyclopaedia. If he was in a bad mood, the class had to sit upright, still and silent, with their reading books open in front of them. Mike had been belted twice. Jinny had shut her eyes so that she wouldn't see it happening. But she had heard it.

"It didn't hurt," said Mike afterwards.

"I would die," said Jinny. "It's not whether it hurts or not. It's letting him hit me. I couldn't."

Jinny missed Petra.

"But you were always fighting," said Mrs. Manders.

"That's what I miss," moaned Jinny. "She made me surer of me. When I saw her fidgeting about with her cold cream and her rollers, and practising the same bit over and over again on the piano, that let me know I'd never be that sort of person."

"I miss her too," agreed Mrs. Manders. "At least she likes her school. I worry about you."

"I worry about Shantih," countered Jinny.

"Are you sure that you wouldn't like us to have a word with Mr. Gorman?"

"That would be THE END," refused Jinny.

On the Friday evening before the Monday half term, Mr. MacKenzie was waiting for them when they rode past his farm.

"Now you'll be having a holiday on Monday," he called to them.

"Half term," answered Mike.

"Three whole days before I have to go back," said Jinny, grinning at the thought. She was going to spend all her time with the ponies. The Shetlands had come to accept Bramble, and hardly bothered to stop grazing when Jinny rode up to them. Only Shantih still moved away, to stand alert and watching – nervous at being separated from the herd, yet too cautious to allow herself to be approached by a human. She would stand whickering to the Shetlands, urging them to follow her out of danger. Jinny hadn't managed to touch her again. If she did ride Bramble closer, Shantih would wheel away and gallop in a wide circle before she stopped at a safe distance – to stand sentinel, ready to be off again should Bramble take another step towards her.

"So you'll be free on Monday?" Mr. MacKenzie inquired.

"Free?" said Mike. "Well, I'm going into Inverburgh with Alec Clark."

"Why?" Jinny asked Mr. MacKenzie.

"I was thinking I might be bringing down the ponies into the wee paddock. I'll be taking a foal or two up to the sale on Wednesday, and I was thinking you might help me with the round-up."

"And Shantih?" cried Jinny.

"Och now, it wouldn't surprise me if she came down too."

"I can't," said Mike.

"I'll ask Ken," said Jinny. "He'll come."

On Monday morning, Jinny and Ken rode over to the farm. The air was sharp with early frost, the mountains charcoal shadows, and the smoke from Finmory rested on the chimney in a vertical plume, like the smoke in a child's drawing.

Jinny sang as she rode. In an hour or two, Shantih
58

would be in Mr. MacKenzie's paddock. Surely she would stop being so afraid, would let Jinny feed her and groom her. Surely she would realise that she wasn't going to be taken back to the circus. "Maybe," Jinny thought, "when the Shetlands go back to the moors, Shantih will stay with me."

"Don't," said Ken. "Stop it."

"Stop what?" said Jinny, turning to scowl at Ken, warning him not to spoil her morning.

"Embroidering your dreams," said Ken. "You'll only be hurt."

Jinny didn't reply. She felt Shantih's warm breath on the palm of her hand as they stood together, watching the Shetlands return to the moor.

In the farmyard, Mr. MacKenzie and Ewan, one of his married sons, were waiting, mounted on two heavy dun Highlands.

"Aye, it's yourselves," greeted Mr. MacKenzie. "Come away now, and we'll have them down in no time. Ewan saw them over by the back of Finmory Beag. We'll circle round and they'll not be knowing what's happening to them till we have them tucked into the paddock."

Mr. MacKenzie led the way out of the yard, shouting to his wife to be ready to shut the yard gate once the ponies were inside. Jinny rode with Ewan, making him laugh as she told him about her attempts to reach Shantih. Ken rode behind the others. He was only there because Jinny had persuaded him to come. He didn't like chasing animals around. He hated to see them panicking from human beings. Ken thought it was one of the basic things that made everything go wrong.

Sheep, grazing stiffly after the night's cold, moved slowly away from them; disturbed crows shuffled their wings and creaked into flight as the riders approached.

They had ridden for about an hour when Mr. MacKenzie reined in his pony, and said that, if Ewan was right, the Shetlands should be over the brow of the next hill.

"We'll come around behind them and just keep them going, easy like. No rushing them. Keep them walking. Once we have them moving in front of us, they'll be no

59

bother. The old yins know there's a touch of oats for them when they come down to the farm."

"What about Shantih?" demanded Jinny. "She'll not know."

"Now don't you be upsetting them all for that warrior. Let her come or not as she likes."

"That's what I'm here for," said Jinny.

"Don't fret yourself," said Ewan. "She'll not be leaving her mates."

They rode over the brow of the hill – and below them was the herd.

"Spread out in a line," said Mr. MacKenzie, as Shantih neighed a warning and the ponies clustered and turned to stare suspiciously at the riders.

"Easy now, easy," warned Mr. MacKenzie, and they walked their mounts slowly down the hill.

Shantih waited, poised for flight, neighing her fear to the Shetlands. But the older mares were used to being rounded up, and continued to graze, only walking slowly forward as the riders approached.

They rode towards the farm, the Shetlands trickling in front of them, while Shantih tore this way and that. Her neck was stretched like a stallion's as she tried to turn the herd; then with a screaming whinny, she would thunder out of sight – only to swing round and come cantering past the Shetlands, nipping and pushing, trying to make them gallop away with her.

"She's like me," Ken thought. "Desperate to be free, yet afraid to leave her friends."

Jinny's face was drawn inwards, her eyes strained as she watched Shantih's wild display.

As they came closer to the farm, Shantih left the herd and galloped away over the hills. Jinny rode looking back over the moor, searching the barren ground for the red gold of the Arab. "Come back. Oh, come back," she willed.

They reached the broad, rutted track that led to the farm. On one side was a stone wall, while the other was open to the moor.

"Watch them here. Don't let them turn. Keep them moving," shouted Mr. MacKenzie.

Ewan rode closer, and the mares broke into a ragged, shuffling trot. Foals shrilled and their mothers answered. The unshod hoofs tapped the earth. Jinny could see Mrs. MacKenzie holding open the yard gate, ready to close it when the ponies were through – but there was still no sign of Shantih.

"Keep them going on. Keep them moving," instructed Mr. MacKenzie.

All the Shetlands were trotting now. The slope down to the farm and the strange horses pressing close behind them fired them with urgency. Jinny rode at the side of the herd, chivvying them on. A mare swerved out from the shaggy mass and Jinny rode at her, swinging her arms, and turned her back.

"Well done!"

Suddenly Shantih came, cantering furiously down from the moor. She circled the herd and was trotting at their head.

Mr. Mackenzie swore. "Watch the horse, she's going to turn them."

As Mr. MacKenzie shouted, Jinny, too, saw what Shantih was trying to do. She urged Bramble forward past the musty sweat of the Shetlands until she was riding close beside Shantih. The Arab snaked her head at Bramble, lips peeled from her teeth, eyes rolling, then she turned and lashed out with both hind hoofs, missing Bramble's shoulder by a hair's breadth.

Jinny stood up in her saddle, shouting at the pitch of her voice, waving her arms – driving Bramble close in to the Arab, forcing her to keep going forward, preventing her from turning and leading the Shetlands back to the moor.

At the yard gate, Shantih saw Mrs. MacKenzie. She stopped dead, tried to rear her way back to freedom, but the press of Shetlands carried her through the gateway and into the yard. The gate clanged shut on the last of the Shetlands. They were all safely inside.

Jinny flopped over Bramble's neck.

"You haven't the red hair for nothing," laughed Mr. MacKenzie.

Ken turned Punch and rode away, sick with himself for

having been part of it. It had been the way he had known it would be – humans hunting terrified animals. He jumped off Punch and, walking at his head, took an apple out of his pocket and shared it with the pony.

Jinny didn't even notice that Ken had gone. She waited impatiently until all the ponies had been driven out of the yard into the paddock. The Shetlands who had been down before went straight to the feeding troughs, while Shantih careered round the paddock.

"She won't jump out, will she?" asked Jinny.

"Not over that fence," said Ewan. "No horse will jump wire as high as that."

Jinny came back to the farm after lunch. All the other ponies had settled down, but Shantih was still raking around. Jinny climbed between the strands of wire and, speaking softly, held out the carrots she had brought for Shantih. The Shetlands clustered round her, nipping and kicking, Jinny pushed through them, chasing them away.

"Shantih," she murmured. "Shantih. Gently now. Gently. I only want to speak to you. There now. There now. Easy now. No one's going to hurt you."

But the Arab hardly seemed to notice that Jinny was there. She was wild and terrified, a caged creature hurtling herself from one end of the paddock to the other. When Jinny did manage to corner her, she stood for a second, trembling, pressing herself against the fence, and then plunged past Jinny and went back to her furious, driven speed.

After about an hour, Mr. MacKenzie came out from the farm and told Jinny to stop upsetting his animals.

"There's no advantage to be chasing her round like that. And it's not myself will be coming to drag you out when one of them gives you the kicking you're asking for."

Reluctantly, Jinny climbed out of the paddock.

"Couldn't you help me catch her? Once I got a halter on her I could groom her."

"Are you completely daft, lass? Give over with your nonsense. You haven't the time or the strength to be tackling that yin. It's a man she'll need after her. Now give over with you. Take a telling and don't be going in there again."

62

Jinny stood by the paddock gate, watching Shantih's useless raging.

"I'm not going to make you go back to a circus. You belong to me now. You've got to trust me. You don't have to trust everyone, but you've got to trust me. Oh, stop being so wild. I've saved you twice. I won't hurt you now."

But the Arab's eyes were fixed on the mountains and freedom.

Jinny came back for the milk later and tried again. Shantih seemed calmer now, and Jinny tried pretending that she wasn't interested in her. She scratched dense-haired Shetland necks, and fed them bits of carrot that were meant for Shantih, never so much as glancing at the chestnut, but no matter how cunning Jinny was, Shantih was always at the other end of the paddock.

Early the next morning, Jinny went back to the farm. Most of the Shetlands were still lying down, or standing more than half asleep. Only Shantih was still on guard. Jinny tried to feed her over the gate, but whenever the Shetlands smelt food they came pushing and shoving, chasing Shantih away from the gate. Jinny climbed into the paddock and trailed pointlessly up and down after the Arab.

After school it was still the same. Ewan was in the yard with his father, deciding on the foals for tomorrow's sale.

"Would I be putting a rope round her for you?" Ewan offered. "Och, I could have her on the ground in a minute. She's needing learnt a lesson. Take the temper out of her."

"Don't you dare," threatened Jinny.

"And how will I sell her with the two broken legs?" asked Mr. MacKenzie.

"You wouldn't sell her. You can't. She's mine."

"Would that be a fact? Well, steady yourself, for I'll not be selling her until the Spring. That's when the toffs will be paying the fancy price for herself."

Jinny waited until it was too dark to see Shantih any longer, then she rode slowly home. Bramble was annoyed at being kept out so late. When Jinny turned him out after his feed, he didn't wait for a carrot the way he usually did, but went off into the night, shouting for Punch.

A lump choked in Jinny's throat. She went back to the

house, saw the light on in the pottery, and, leaving her school bag at the back door, she went to see who was there.

Ken was sitting at the wheel, doodling with a lump of clay. The grey hearth rug of Kelly opened unsuspected eyelids to examine Jinny through amber eyes.

"Not on?" asked Ken.

Jinny couldn't speak. She sat down on the ledge beside Ken.

"Nobody love you?"

"Well, they don't," said Jinny. "Even Bramble didn't want a carrot. It's all right for you. Look at all this . . ." And Jinny gestured at the shelves already beginning to fill up with pots – some glazed and decorated, some still grey and dead, waiting to be fired. "You've done all this. Put new windows in . . ." Jinny went on pointing, to the large window which now made up one side of the pottery. "And the roof and all the gardening. Daddy's got his book. Petra loves her beastly school . . ."

"Poor Jinny."

"Well, it's true. I can't get near Shantih. She's there in the paddock and I still can't catch her. What am I going to do?"

"People are so impatient. Not only want, but want everything NOW."

Ken treadled the wheel, and the clay slimed into life under his long, bony fingers. In his hip pocket was the cheque from his parents. It had come direct from his father's bank. "This way they know that I'm not starving to death and they don't even have to write to me," Ken had said.

Seeing the cheque, Jinny felt a swell of conscience – for that would be worse, so much worse. But she pushed the thought away from her – she couldn't allow herself to think about it at the moment.

"What am I going to do?" she demanded again. Nothing in the world mattered, except finding a way to tame Shantih. It was worse seeing her so close and still not being able to reach her. "How can I make her trust me?"

"Make?" echoed Ken. "*Make* her trust you? It's the making she doesn't trust, and why should she? You'd need

64

years to recover if someone had treated you the way she's been treated."

"Mr. MacKenzie will turn her loose again tomorrow," said Jinny. "I haven't got years."

Ken treadled the wheel into a blur of speed. Jinny had to wait until he stopped it revolving, sliced off the pot and lifted it delicately on to a bat.

"There was a book," he said. "I remember the photographs. A woman who had trained wild horses in the Argentine. Going up to them with her hands behind her back, breathing love and trust into their nostrils. Tremendous."

"Yes," said Jinny. "That's what I want to know. How to tell her I love her. That she doesn't need to be afraid."

"Get the book if you like. It would give you the patter. But you know it all yourself, if you'd only give yourself the chance. Stop grabbing."

Jinny looked up the number of the County Library and phoned. A girl's voice answered, and Jinny did her best to explain what she wanted.

"I know the one," said the girl. "It's a fairly old one. Might just be in reserve stock. Hold on, and I'll see if I can find it."

Jinny held on, fingers crossed, until the girl came back.

"Hullo?"

"Have you got it?"

"You're in luck. I've got a copy and it's the right one. It's got the photographs in it."

"Oh, thank you," cried Jinny.

"Will you come into Inverburgh for it?"

"I must have it tomorrow," said Jinny. "But I can't get to Inverburgh. I'll be at Glenbost."

"The Mobile Library goes through Ardtallon tomorrow," suggested the girl. "I could give it to Thomas and you could collect it there. He'll be at Ardtallon round about two."

"Where's Ardtallon?"

"Oh, only about four miles from Glenbost. The far side from Inverburgh. What's your name?"

Jinny told her, and put the phone down slowly. She had to have the book. If the author had been able to tame wild

65

horses, surely it would tell her how to tame Shantih. If she was going to Ardtallon tomorrow afternoon, she would need to play truant. Jinny stood with her hand still on the smooth comforting shape of the receiver. Her father was going to see the owner of a craft shop, who was interested in buying some of the pottery, so there was no chance of him driving to Ardtallon. She couldn't ask Ken to walk there. She would need to go herself.

Jinny thought about Mr. Gorman's rage. She thought about the belt. But it didn't matter. It was for Shantih. Once she had the book it would tell her what to do.

CHAPTER EIGHT

Straight, solid torrents of rain blotted out the mountains, joining the low clouds to the grey-green land. The village of Glenbost was closed in a paperweight of rain. Through the schoolroom windows, Jinny could see nothing but rain – the first stage of another Flood. She finished the day's problems, ruled a neat line under them, and took her exercise book out to Mr. Gorman's desk. He was doing a crossword puzzle and didn't look up.

She went back to her desk, noticing little things that normally she would have missed – knots in the scrubbed wooden floor that suddenly looked like Shantih, the wooden grain flowing like her mane; a mummified wasp that had lain in a windowsill corner since the summer, and a gust of peat reek from the clothes of a boy who dropped his pencil and bent to pick it up.

Jinny sat down next to Dolina's rejecting back. Just by glancing at Dolina's back, Jinny could tell the mood she was in. She pretended to herself that she didn't care if nobody spoke to her, but really she did. All the time she had to be on her guard against the other children in case she should forget – and try to speak to them, giving them the chance to stare at her, then turn away giggling, leaving Jinny with awkward hands and feet, not knowing what to do with herself while they laughed at her.

The rain drummed on the roof, overflowed from a broken rone, and cascaded over the window. Jinny ruled the cage of lines that would dissect Mr. Gorman's chalky scribble into clauses. In another hour it would be half-past twelve, and they would stop for lunch. That was when Jinny had to escape. She swallowed hard, not allowing herself to pick at the thought. She was going to do it and that was that.

She had seen Mr. MacKenzie loading the ponies for the sale that morning, as they rode past on their way to school.

"You'll have said goodbye to your fancy horse?" he had shouted through the downpour.

"What?" yelled back Jinny, lifting the flap of her sou'-wester.

"I'll be putting them back on the hill when I've got these aboard."

"Oh no!" cried Jinny. "No! You can't. You mustn't! I didn't know. Please don't let them go until I see her to-night. Oh, Mr. MacKenzie, promise. Please."

"They'll have my good ground churned into a midden, penned in on a day like this."

"Well, just Shantih. Keep Shantih?"

"Give over plaguing me with your nonsense."

"Please," demanded Jinny.

"Until this evening, then. And that's final."

"That'll be enough. I'm going to get . . ." Jinny had stopped herself just in time, remembering that if she told nobody, nobody would know. "Thank you, Mr. MacKenzie," she had shouted as she trotted after Mike.

Because it was so wet, there were more children than usual sitting on the cloakroom pipes, eating their sandwiches. They munched silently, staring at Jinny as she buttoned herself into her oilskins, pulled on her wellingtons and collected Bramble's tack from its corner.

"Are you riding in this?" Mike asked.

"I've got a headache," Jinny told him, loudly enough for the others to hear. "I'm going for a ride to see if it will help. If it doesn't, I'm going home."

Mike looked dubiously at his sister, knowing she was lying, and guessing it was something to do with Shantih. "Have you told Mr. Gorman?"

But Jinny, clutching saddle and bridle, was sploshing her way down the path.

Both ponies were standing inside their lean-to shed. Jinny squeezed between them and had Bramble's bridle on before he realised what was happening. A few minutes later she was riding him back up the road to Finmory. Eyes watched her from the cloakroom window. Mrs. Simpson called from her shop doorway to ask what was wrong.

"I'm not feeling well," Jinny shouted back. "I'm going home."

Bramble trotted briskly forward, his ears pricked, willing and bright, despite the weather. He thought he was being ridden home to the feed that was always waiting for him when he got back to Finmory.

"There's a good pony," encouraged Jinny, clapping his neck, her hand sinking into the wet sponge of his winter coat. "On you go," and she hurried him out of sight of Glenbost.

Once she was absolutely certain that the last croft was safely hidden behind a hill, Jinny halted Bramble and took out of her pocket the diagram she had copied from her father's Ordnance Survey map. She studied it, then carefully returned the sodden piece of paper to her pocket. She was planning to cut across the moor behind Glenbost. Marked on the Ordnance Survey was a dotted line that ran across the moor and joined the road about a mile from Ardtallon. A dotted line meant a footpath. It had been perfectly clear on the map. Bramble tugged at his bit, turning his head against the rain, fretting irritably at the pointless delay. The moors were desolate under the downpour, the familiar landmarks of the hills were hidden by the mist. In the flat, grey landscape, there was no sign of the confident dotted line that would lead them to Ardtallon.

"We'll need to go across country," Jinny told Bramble. "Cross country," she said again loudly. It made her think of explorers striking out into the unknown, of intrepid horses and riders tackling the house-sized obstacles at Badminton. "And all we've got to do is ride across a bit of moor." She gathered up the slimy reins, kicked her wellington heels hard against Bramble's sides, and tried to turn him off the road.

Bramble remained a solid, immovable bulk. Jinny's heels bounced ineffectively against his wooden sides. She pulled at the reins, trying to upset his foursquare balance. Bramble went into reverse. Jinny kicked and shouted, terrified that a car would come past and find them there, and in some way organize them back to school. Bramble suddenly flung himself sideways. Jinny lost a stirrup and clutched at a handful of mane as the pony bucked, and, head down, charged for home.

For a second, Jinny clung to the pony, kippered over his neck, certain that she was coming off. But the friction of her oilskin trousers against the wet saddle leather gave her a moment of purchase. Somehow, she pushed herself back into the saddle, struggled to recapture her dangling stirrups and hauled in the slippery reins. She had stopped feeling cold or wet; stopped thinking about what would happen if Mr. Gorman found out; she had only one thought in her head – to get Bramble to Ardtallon in time to meet the library van.

Despite Jinny's efforts to slow him down, Bramble charged on.

"Right," Jinny thought. She found her second stirrup, dug her knees against the saddle and swung Bramble round off the road and across the moor. He tried to stop, to fight his way back to the road, but Jinny had caught him by surprise and forced him to keep on galloping. "Go on, go on," she urged. "Get on with you." Ardtallon was somewhere to the left of Glenbost, and that was where they were going. They hadn't time to worry about dotted lines on maps. She forced Bramble on into the grey nothingness.

One minute they were cantering over firm ground. The next, Jinny felt Bramble's quarters sink, and his neck and shoulders rear above her. Too late to do anything to stop herself, she fell backwards. She rolled clear of the pony and scrabbled on to hands and knees, to see Bramble with his forelegs dug into firm ground, struggling to free himself from a bog. Jinny screamed, and stumbled to grab his reins.

She pulled frantically at the pony's bridle, shouting at

69

him, urging him to free himself. Bramble's eyes stared from his head as he clutched the solid ground with hooked fore-legs, struggling violently. There was a squelching explosion as he burst free. He stood with his head down, fighting for breath, like a point-to-point horse in the winner's enclo-sure.

Jinny waited until he had recovered, then remounted. Covered in mud herself, she hardly noticed the state of the saddle or the pony. She knew that she had been mad to gallop a pony over treacherous moorland on a day like this. Bright behind her eyes was the frozen frame of Bramble fighting to free himself.

"If he hadn't known what to do himself, there was noth-ing you could have done to save him," chided Jinny's con-science. "You would have killed him."

"If you don't get a move on, you'll be too late. The library van won't wait. You won't get your book. Mr. MacKenzie will turn Shantih out on to the moors again. You won't have another chance," warned another voice in Jinny's head.

With a filthy hand, Jinny pushed back dripping rats' tails of hair from her face. She knew which voice she always listened to in the end. She gritted her teeth and forced Bramble to gallop, watching for the fluorescent warning of the green scum that marked the bogs.

It was Bramble who found the path that was the dotted line on the map. Jinny had been completely lost. Even when they reached its safety, Jinny wasn't certain which way led to Ardtallon. She let the reins fall on Bramble's neck. He turned instantly towards Finmory. Jinny swung him round and, ignoring his protests, pushed him into a trot and then a canter. She had no idea what time it was. She only knew that it seemed much longer than an hour since she had left school.

"Please, please let the library van still be there," she prayed, as Bramble's hooves clattered along the road to Ardtallon.

When they reached the first of the Ardtallon crofts, crouched under the rain, Jinny looked around anxiously for any sign of the van, haunted by the dread that she would be too late, that the library driver would have been and gone. Then she saw it, a bulky, dark green van parked in front of the village shop.

As Jinny approached, a woman clutching books under an umbrella came out of the van and a man began to fold up the steps that led up to the door of the vehicle.

"Wait!" Jinny yelled. "Wait for me."

The man and the woman stared as Jinny, oilskins flapping, rode down on them. She floundered off Bramble's back and caught a glimpse of their reflection in the shop window. Jinny was covered in streaks and rivulets of mud, and Bramble was clotted with lumps of black peat and plastered with slime.

"I am glad you're still here," Jinny exclaimed, smiling, expecting the man to smile back at her, but he only stood in the doorway of his library van, staring down at her, waiting. The woman tutted under her umbrella. Jinny tried smiling at her, but Dolina's expressionless cod eyes looked blankly back at her. Jinny's stomach rolled. She must be Dolina's mother.

"You've got a book for me," Jinny said, turning back to the man. "I phoned up the Central Library last night and the girl there said she'd put it on the library van for me today."

"I'll not be knowing you?" said the man, as the woman tutted off into the rain.

Jinny didn't see that it mattered – most of the assistants in the Stopton library hadn't known her.

"You'll not be a member of the library?"

"No, we've just come to live here. I'll join now."

"What's your name and address?" asked the man, taking a form out of a drawer.

"Jinny Manders," Jinny told him, peering into the van at the tempting shelves of brightly-jacketed books. The man was leaning on a counter that separated the cabin of the van from the library shelves. At one end of the counter was a pile of books. The top book had a slip of paper sticking out of it. In scrawled capitals Jinny read, 'MANDERS. PHONE CALL. ARDTALLON STOP'.

"That's it," Jinny cried in delight. "That's it. You've got it. That's my book – the one on top there."

Jinny's grin spread from ear to ear. Even if she got the

belt tomorrow it had been worth it. The book would tell her how to breathe trust and gentleness into Shantih; how to let her know that she would never hurt her, never let anyone else terrify her, never ever again.

"Address?" demanded the man, his features solid as a carved figurehead.

"Finmory House," said Jinny.

The man put down his pen, tore the form into two pieces and dropped them into a waste paper basket.

"In that case," he said, "you're taking no books from my van. I might have known from the sight of you. Twenty pounds worth of books the last lot of hippies from Finmory stole from the County Library. Books that they were on at me to get specially for them, and never a one of them returned."

"But they had nothing to do with us!" exclaimed Jinny. "Nothing at all. We never even met them. Finmory was empty when Daddy bought it."

"Not another of my books goes out to anyone coming from Finmory."

"They're not *your* books," retorted Jinny. "They're for everyone to borrow. You MUST give it to me."

"For everyone to borrow that brings them back. And if you were from Buckingham Palace I wouldn't be harding over one of my books to a tink like yourself, standing in the road shouting at me."

Jinny listened in blank astonishment, slowly realising that he really wasn't going to let her have the book. She dropped Bramble's reins, sprang into the van and made a grab at the book. Her hand closed on it a fraction before the man gripped her wrist and forced her to drop it.

"Don't you dare be pushing your way into my van. Get out with you and back to school where you belong."

With his hand on the scruff of Jinny's oilskin, he propelled her back into the road. The van door was banged shut, and in seconds the van was swaying down the road, taking Jinny's book with it.

"You suppurating slug, you ponging pig – you liverwort!" Jinny did a war dance of hate in the deserted road.

As she rode home, following the track over the moors,

72

she could still hardly believe that anyone could have been as mean as the driver of the library van.

Jinny reached home without being seen. She left Bramble in his stable munching down his feed, then, taking off her oilskins, which were pointless now since her clothes seemed to be soaking, she ran back to the farm. She knew Shantih was still there, for she had heard the mare's screeching whinny as they had ridden past.

The Arab was standing alone in the middle of the paddock. Mr. MacKenzie had kept his word.

"Shantih," Jinny called. "Shantih." And the mare came plunging to the gate. The bright gold of her coat was darkened by the rain to a liverish purple, her legs were sleeked into bony skeletons, her mane was laid flat against her neck and the wisp of her forelock was plastered down her face. She pushed at the gate, thrusting her weight against it, clattering it with frantic forehooves, a crazy mare for the storm witch to ride.

Jinny paused, knowing that on a day like this it would be more impossible than usual to get near Shantih. She thought she heard the farm door being opened, and knew that if it was Mr. MacKenzie he would want to turn Shantih back on to the moor.

Trying to remember everything that Ken had told her about the methods the woman had used to tame wild horses, Jinny ran up the side of the paddock and climbed through the fence.

"Shantih," she called again.

The Arab turned towards her but stood still, unwilling to leave the gate.

"Hands behind my back," Jinny told herself. "So she knows I'm not trying to catch her. Breathe slowly and gently, hold my face out towards her."

Jinny moved slowly, placing each foot carefully in the mud. Usually, by this time, Shantih would have galloped off to the other end of the paddock.

Jinny stood still, murmuring soft, comforting reassurance. She took another step forward – and another. Stood still again, blowing through her nose, speaking to the horse with her breath. She had stopped trying to remember the things that Ken had told her from the book. He had been

73

right, she didn't need anyone to tell her what to do; she knew, had always known. Breathing was the way to calm horses. It was the way they spoke to each other. Spoken words were only breath chopped into little pieces, and animals didn't need to do that. They breathed.

Shantih stretched out her neck, reaching her head out towards Jinny. Her rain-carved head was delicate and precise as a wild flower. She took a hesitant step towards Jinny.

Slowly, lovingly, Jinny breathed. She didn't let her excitement come up to the surface of her mind. All her attention had to stay on her breathing, as it created a gossamer thread that drew Shantih towards her.

Hesitant, flinching, her every nerve tensed to spring back, Shantih took another step towards Jinny.

"What's up with you now? Would you look at you, standing there like a dooley in the pouring rain."

The disharmony of Mr. MacKenzie's roar broke the spell of breath. Shantih flipped into the opposite, terrified and wild again, she reared.

"No. Oh no!" shouted Jinny, but she yelled at the farmer for spoiling everything, not at the horse rearing menacingly above her. Shantih's foreleg moved more swiftly than Jinny could see. She only felt the blow on her shoulder that sent her sprawling into the mud, heard Mr. MacKenzie's yells as he came dashing to the gate, pelting Shantih with gravel he had grabbed from the yard.

"Are you still with us?" he demanded.

Jinny slithered to her feet. "Of course," she said crossly.

"The brute could have had you dead." And Mr. MacKenzie fired another round of stones to where Shantih tore up and down at the far fence. "Now get that gate open and let's be seeing the last of her."

"No . . ." said Jinny, but Mr. MacKenzie was already dragging the gate wide.

"Come on then. Let's be shut of you," he shouted at the horse.

Jinny stood watching helplessly as Shantih charged into the yard, spooked and shied at the outbuildings, then saw the open gateway that led on to the moors. She went high stepping through it, electric with fear, then stretched into speed, low to the ground, desperate to find the Shetlands again, to get as far away as possible from everything to do with humans.

"Oh, why did you have to come just then?" cried Jinny. "Why just at that moment?"

"That's a fine way to be thanking me for saving your life," said Mr. MacKenzie.

"But why?" cried Jinny. "Why? Just when she was getting to know me."

CHAPTER NINE

"My mother saw her at the library van yesterday afternoon," Dolina announced the next morning.

Jinny wasn't in the least surprised. She had been expecting it. There had been a lot of trouble at home last night. First of all over the state of Jinny's clothes, and, when they had found out where she had been, about the undesirability of such behaviour.

"But I'd done all my work for the day," Jinny had defended herself. "All I would have been doing would have been sitting up straight with that reading book open in front of me. And I've read it fifty thousand times already."

"When Mr. Gorman asks where you were, you've to tell him the truth," said Jinny's father.

"He might not ask," Jinny had replied hopefully.

Now, sitting next to Dolina's back, Jinny didn't feel so optimistic. She hadn't slept much last night because of the pain in her shoulder where Shantih had kicked her. Her parents hadn't found out about that yet. Jinny had examined her shoulder in her dressing-table mirror. When she prodded it experimentally, the pain had stabbed down her arm, making the bedroom walls swing about her, so that Jinny had decided that it was better to leave it alone. This morning it hurt if she even moved her arm.

"Good morning, boys and girls."

"Good morning, Mr. Gorman," responded the class as their teacher walked in.

The boys saluted and the girls curtsied. Jinny stretched

out her left arm to balance herself and the pain ripped through her, draining the blood from her face and leaving her panting for breath as she sat down again. If her shoulder didn't get any better she would need to tell her mother and risk hospitals and injections.

When Mr. Gorman reached Jinny's name in the register, he stopped and stared at her.

"So you've returned to the fold, Jennifer Manders." The class waited expectantly. "Have you brought a note?"

"No," said Jinny.

"Stand up, girl, when you're speaking to me."

Jinny stood up, keeping her arm close to her side, taking care not to move it.

"And may I enquire why not?" asked Mr. Gorman. "Come out here."

Jinny went out. She was thinking hard about Shantih, about the moment when the Arab had been so close to her – not tricked, but coming towards her of her own free will.

"And where were you yesterday afternoon?"

Jinny thought about Saturday, when she would go up the moors and find Shantih again, when there would be no Mr. MacKenzie to spoil everything.

"I'm waiting."

"I went to Ardtallon to get a book from the library van."

"A book for yourself?"

Jinny nodded. "I had to go."

"Indeed," said Mr. Gorman. "Indeed. You had to go? You had to play truant? You had to tell lies? Because that's what you did, that's exactly what you did."

The scarlet temper flooded over his high-bridged nose, flushed around his peering eyes and bloomed over the bald dome of his head.

Jinny looked straight at him. She knew he was going to belt her, and now that it was actually happening she only wanted to get it over; to be back at her desk away from the staring children.

Mr. Gorman took the strap out of his desk and laid it on the lid in front of him.

"Hold out your hand and let this be a lesson to you. No more jaunting off whenever the notion takes you."

Jinny held out her right hand.

"The other hand, girl," ordered Mr. Gorman. "You'll be telling me next that you can't hold a pencil."

Jinny lifted her left hand about six inches from her side and gasped aloud with pain.

"I can't. I've hurt my shoulder."

"Indeed, indeed," syruped Mr. Gorman. "Now don't tell me any more of your lies. Hold out your hand."

"I can't . . ."

Mr. Gorman made a grab at her hand. Jinny heard the scream that rang around the classroom, but didn't connect it with herself. In the far distance, she heard Mike shouting at Mr. Gorman to leave his sister alone, and then she was falling down and down, the classroom walls flowing outward like a science fiction nightmare.

Jinny came to sitting at a desk, with her head between her knees. She struggled to sit up. "It wasn't because he was going to hit me. It wasn't. I've hurt my shoulder but I'm all right now. I'm quite all right."

When Mr. Manders got Jinny to Inverburgh General Hospital, the doctor there didn't agree. He was very annoyed that Jinny hadn't been brought in the night before.

"The muscle is badly torn, and I dare say the bone is cracked. We'll know after the X-ray."

But the bone wasn't damaged, so they strapped Jinny up with rolls of elastoplast and let her go home.

"It would have to be my left shoulder. If it had been my right arm, I could have stayed off school."

"Why didn't you tell me?" said her mother.

"You were cross enough with me as it was."

"But only because you do such irresponsible things. I'm only cross because I love you."

"I know," said Jinny. "But I can't remember it all the time. When you're cross I just think you're cross. And when Shantih is all wild and mad and won't let me near her, I know it's because of the way she's been treated. She didn't mean to kick me. We have to remember that."

"I'll say this for you," laughed Mrs. Manders. "You are

gifted at turning a conversation round to suit your own ends."

"A few more inches and she'd have kicked your face," said Petra, when she came home on Friday night to be impressed by Jinny's strapped shoulder.

"All I've done is twist my shoulder a bit," Jinny said to Ken. "It's stopped hurting. Couldn't have been serious when all they did was put sticking plaster on it."

"You make it sound as if they stuck on a Band Aid," said Ken.

"The fuss everyone's made. Even Mr. Gorman asked if it was O.K. But no one wants to hear about Shantih. No one wants to know about her. And I'm all smashed up about her. As if I'd been put into a blender and turned on at Hi Speed. I don't know what to do next."

November was grey and wet. A wind moaned in from the sea, driving the rain. Day after day, Mike and Jinny fought their way through pouring rain to and from Glenbost.

"My feet are webbing over," complained Mike. "Wish I were old enough to go with Petra. It's O.K. for her. Special minibus on a Monday morning, and brought home to the door on a Friday night."

"I couldn't be away all week," said Jinny. "I couldn't leave Shantih."

"Wouldn't make much difference if you were on the moon."

"Would," said Jinny. "She might need me."

But the words sounded hollow, even in Jinny's ears. The first Saturday after Shantih had been in Mr. MacKenzie's paddock, Jinny had got up at seven and set off up the hills to find the ponies. She didn't ride because she couldn't think what she would do with Bramble while she was breathing to Shantih. It was after dark before Jinny got back home.

"And about time too," said her father. "Another quarter of an hour and Ken and I would have been up those mountains searching for you. How can I be expected to write when I'm wondering where you are all the time?"

"I didn't realise it was so late until it started getting dark. Then I went the wrong way."

78

"You do know, don't you, that Mr. MacKenzie, who was born here, would think twice before he went wandering over those hills alone at night?"

Jinny knew. She had been scared, wandering around, trying to find her way back; had felt panic breathing on the back of her neck, forcing her to run. Jumping down from a rock, she had landed on a soft patch, and for seconds she hadn't been able to wrench her feet free – had felt the sucking mouth of the bog trying to pull her down.

Standing in the safety of Finmory kitchen, Jinny shuddered. One of Mr. MacKenzie's favourite stories was about a Shetland that had been sucked down into a bog and died of starvation. When Mr. MacKenzie found her body, only her head was left above the emerald slime.

"Double pneumonia, that's what you'll have next," predicted Mrs. Manders. "On you go, and have a really hot bath while I'm getting you some supper."

Jinny obeyed her mother gladly, shutting the door on Petra's questions about whether or not she had managed to get near Shantih – for in her whole day's wanderings, Jinny had only glimpsed the Arab once.

After three more weekends – all equally fruitless – Jinny was on the edge of despair.

"But what else can I do?" she asked Ken one evening, when they were sitting together in the pottery – Jinny half-heartedly making a coil pot which she knew she would never finish. Making pots was too slow for her. She liked decorating other people's, but Ken said that was cheating.

"November is the hopeless month," said Ken, who was examining dishes that had come out of the kiln that afternoon. "Everything is hopeless in November."

"You're telling me," said Jinny. "How can you love someone the way I love Shantih and not be able to reach her? She could be in the stable. I've got it all ready for her."

Years ago, when Finmory had been a farm, one of the outbuildings had been a feed house and stables. Now the Manders kept their bins of oats and nuts, and bales of hay, and the ponies' tack in it. Joined on to the feed house were two stalls, in fairly good order, where Punch and Bramble were fed and groomed. Opposite the stalls was a large loose box. It had been filled with rubble and rotting planks of wood. Helped by Mike, Jinny had cleared it out and put down a thick bed of straw.

"Thought that was for Punch and Bramble."

"They don't need to be inside. The Shetlands are O.K. as well. But not an Arab. An Arab can't survive out on the moors all winter. They all hate wind and rain, like this, but it's much worse for Shantih. She hasn't got a thick winter coat to protect her the way the others have."

"Maybe when it's colder she'll come down for hay," suggested Ken.

"She won't," prophesied Jinny. "Not Shantih. She'll die up there on the moors rather than come near humans." And she squashed the beginnings of her pot back into a lump of clay.

"Like the rest of us," agreed Ken. "Wants her own way."

He was moving the pots about on the shelves, trying to find space for the newly-fired ones. He lifted each dish with consideration and care, without any hurry or sense of irritation. It was as if, under his hands, the mugs and coffee pots, bowls and vases agreed to move closer together and accept the newcomers.

The wind flattened the rain against the window, whistled through cracks and crevices, fingered at the roof, searching for weaknesses – driving rain between the old slates and the new ones that Ken and Mr. Manders had added in the summer.

"Perhaps if you'd left her alone," suggested Ken, "she would have settled by now. But you can't leave her alone, can you?"

"No," said Jinny. "I can't."

She threw the lump of clay into a bin and left Ken to himself, surrounded by the curved shapes of the pots, winking and gleaming in the light of the bare electric bulb. They were already sold. At the end of the month they were to be packed up and taken to a craft shop in Inverburgh.

The wind grabbed the door, slamming it shut behind Jinny. She paused for a moment, then launched herself out into the dark. As she struggled back to the house, the wind buffeted her from side to side. She leant against it, felt it packed solid – almost like water into which she could have plunged and flown. The furious crests of the waves flashed whitely on the horizon, and behind Jinny the mountains tightened their roots against the force of the gale.

The kitchen door was bolted. Jinny banged with both fists against it until her mother opened it and she blundered into the warmth and light.

"We had to bolt it to keep it shut," explained Mrs. Manders. "What a night! It's the worst we've had yet."

They went through to the front room.

"We ought to be out with lanterns," said Mike, looking up from his homework. "Luring ships to their doom on the rocks."

"Feel free," said Jinny.

"Ken still out in the pottery?" asked Mr. Manders.

"Think he's just coming in," said Jinny, crouched over the fire which swirled and gusted. The wind howled under the door, lifting the carpet. The heavy curtains swayed and the house was full of creaks and groans. If you listened carefully under all the other noises, you could hear the thunderous, grating boom of the sea crashing up Finmory Bay.

"If it's like this tomorrow, we'll not be able to go to school," said Mike.

Normally such ideas were squashed at once, but tonight neither their father nor mother bothered to disagree.

"Wish he'd come back in," said Mr. Manders, lifting the curtain to stare out into the glistening blackness. "Think I'll go and get him. Not a night for man nor beast."

"But Shantih is out in it," Jinny said, and she was glad that the Arab had the Shetlands for company. Probably they had survived much worse storms than this one.

When Mr. Manders and Ken came back in, they all sat around the fire, roasting potatoes in the ashes. Mike caught Jinny's eye and grinned, drawing her attention to the clock on the mantelpiece. It was almost eleven o'clock. Jinny grinned back, but underneath she felt uneasy. No matter how hard she tried not to, all she was doing was listening to the storm gathering strength outside.

It was after midnight when Mrs. Manders, at last, suggested that they might as well all go to bed and try to sleep.

Jinny lay curled in bed, her ears straining and her neck tense. Usually she loved being in bed, warm and cosy, while the wind raged outside, but tonight the wind was trying to get inside. It struck against the house as if it were a solid force, a sledgehammer of air. Every time it struck the window, Jinny's heart seemed to hesitate, waiting for the glass to splinter and let the monster into her room. The darkness was full of bangs and thuds, as loose objects, or anything which the wind could tear from its foundations, went batting through the night.

"It must stop soon," Jinny thought. "It can't get any worse. It's a hurricane. A typhoon." And she saw Finmory sucked up and spiralled into space. To pick up a house and fling it away would be nothing to a wind like this. It rode in from the ocean, raged up the flat fields in front of Finmory, thudded against the stone walls and broke into waves of fury to swell, moaning and screaming, over the moors.

Jinny heard her father go downstairs again. She got up too, dressed, and followed him down. Soon they were all standing around the Aga, drinking coffee.

"Keep back from the windows," cautioned Mr. Manders.

"Should we go out to see Bramble and Punch?" Jinny asked, hoping that no one would suggest she go alone.

"They'll be fine," said her mother. "Tucked in under the hedge, I expect."

"You couldn't stand in this," said Mr. Manders. "No, I mean it. I can remember . . ."

They never heard what he could remember, for, as he spoke, a terrifying surge of wind burst over the house. Mrs. Manders swore afterwards that she had seen the walls tremble. Pictures fell to the floor, ornaments leapt from shelves, and the light swung in crazy circles. Somewhere outside there was a thunderous explosion.

"The pottery!" yelled Ken. He sprang to the door, wrenched it open and, with Mr. Manders at his side, ran into the night.

"You're not to go with them," Mrs. Manders shouted, but Jinny was already through the door. Ken grabbed her

82

hand, and they raced together through a world without gravity, where solid objects zoomed and soared, where invisible talons ripped the earth.

"But what's happened to it?" shouted Jinny, standing oblivious of the tumult around her, staring at the unbelievable mound of rubble that only a few hours ago had been the pottery.

"But I'd sold the pots," groaned Mr. Manders, "and I've spent the money."

It was as if the destruction of the pottery had satisfied the wind, for only an hour or so afterwards the gale had blown itself out, and the wind that snuffled over the scattered debris was tamed and guilty.

Mike and Jinny were allowed to have the day off school. "Seeing you were up all night," said Mrs. Manders. "Now that doesn't mean that any of us who might be thinking of going up the moors to look for a certain horse will be allowed to do that."

"But . . ."

"No. Tomorrow's Friday. You can wait till Saturday."

Jinny was helping Ken to drag branches out of the drive when she saw the postman's red van.

"Letter for K. Dawson, addressed here."

Jinny ran to take it from him. It wasn't Ken's typewritten envelope containing his monthly cheque, but a cheap brown one, fingermarked, and addressed in smudged biro. Jinny didn't like the look of it. It reminded her that Ken had been on probation. The thought made her glance away from Ken when she gave the letter to him.

Ken put it in his pocket without opening it, but Jinny knew by his silence at lunchtime that he had read it. He ate his fruit and raw vegetables – then sprang abruptly from the table.

"I'm going down the beach by myself," he announced abrasively, and was gone.

"Something wrong?" Mr. Manders asked.

His wife said she didn't know what it could be, and Jinny said nothing.

"Thought we might have had a proper look at the pottery. See what sort of state the kiln is in," grumbled Mr. Manders. "The roof beams must have been riddled with dry rot to come down like that. A ghost of a chance that some of our stuff in the bottom shelves might have survived. But I'd need Ken to help me lift the roof off."

"He might not be long," soothed Mrs. Manders.

"Don't see what he had to go marching off like that for. Not today. You'd think he'd care. Lots of the pots were his. Some nice stuff. Better than some of my pathetics."

Ken didn't come back until after seven. He came into the front room where the Manders were sitting around the fire.

"You look frozen," welcomed Mrs. Manders. "Come and warm yourself."

Ken's lean face was pinched and tense, his nose sharp with the cold, his green eyes, opaque pebbles, looked around scornfully at the firelit room.

"I'm O.K. here," he said, and sat down in an armchair in the far corner of the room. He folded his legs to sit cross-legged, and held up a sliver of sea-bleached wood, concentrating on the grain of the wood, cutting himself off from them.

Jinny, kneeling in front of the fire, tried to go on with the pony book she was reading, but suddenly it didn't seem to matter whether Kirsty won the show-jumping or not. She knew something was wrong with Ken. "It's to do with that letter," she thought, and wished she could say something that would let Ken know that they all wanted him here, that living at Finmory was better because he was with them, that, if they could, they wanted to help him.

"Wouldn't you like some supper?" asked Mrs. Manders, which was her way of saying what Jinny wanted to say.

Ken didn't answer.

"Thought you might have given me a hand to try and lift the pottery roof," said Mr. Manders.

"Oh, don't go on at him," Jinny thought, groping desperately for words to cover over Ken's silence.

"So that's what you thought," said Ken, staring straight at Mr. Manders. "You're pretty good at the thinking. Yes, I'll give you that. You've got it together here, haven't you? All safe and blanket-stitched round the edges. You've forgotten Stopton even exists."

"Ken!" protested Mrs. Manders, while Jinny sat frozen, her eyes fixed on the meaningless black print of her book.

"Oh, you're writing about it O.K. And you'll make money out of it because you're pretty quick with your thinking. But what about the ones that are still living in it? What about them? Existing in rotten, stinking derries or back ends. Doesn't matter much, does it? They're not good enough to think, or, if they do start thinking for themselves, the police soon interfere."

"You know I see it that way too," said Mr. Manders. "But I could do nothing, Ken. I had to get out. What I'm trying to say in my book is what you're shouting now. I'm shouting in my book. And if it's published, more people will hear me. Some of them may even open their eyes and see."

"Is that a fact?" said Ken. "Big deal."

Jinny starfished her fingers through the pile of the rug and heard Mike swallow gulpingly.

"If I'd stayed on in Stopton any longer I'd have gone mad or deaf. Started using labels – yobs, vandals, muggers."

"Well, that's how you see us, isn't it?" challenged Ken.

"You think that?" asked Mr. Manders.

"Think?" said Ken. "No, I don't think. I'm one of them. I know."

"Don't," pleaded Jinny. "Don't. You don't mean it."

"And I'll tell you what I know," continued Ken, ignoring Jinny. "You're the same as my parents, and you make me sick."

Ken leapt up and dashed out of the room.

The next afternoon, when Jinny and Mike came out of school, Ken was waiting for them at the gate of the ponies' field. His pack was at his feet and he was holding Kelly by a length of string.

"What's wrong?" cried Jinny, running towards him. "What's the matter?" she asked again, although she had known from the moment she had seen him standing there that he was leaving.

"I'm splitting," said Ken. "Keep an eye on Kelly for a
85

day or two in case he tries to follow me." And he gave Kelly's string to Jinny.

"But why? Why? Have you told Dad?"

"Take joy," said Ken, lifting his open hand to Jinny, and before Mike had reached the gate, Ken was walking down the road without a backward glance.

CHAPTER TEN

Mr. and Mrs. Wright and their two daughters, Susan and Belinda, friends of the Manders from Stopton, came to stay for Christmas.

Petra, who had been very friendly with Susan Wright, was dashing round the house making last-minute adjustments to paper chains and holly before the Wrights arrived, and wishing aloud that Mr. MacKenzie nadn't given them their Christmas tree and then they could have bought a silver one from Boots.

"They don't make all this mess and they look really nice. Nobody has real trees nowadays."

"The Wrights had a real one last year," Jinny reminded her.

"And Susan loathed it."

"She would," thought Jinny. "And Belinda would hate it, too."

Belinda Wright had been in Jinny's class. Like Susan, she was pink marshmallow plump, with flaxen hair and wide blue eyes that leaked glycerine tears when Belinda wanted her own way. At Stopton, Jinny had done her best to avoid her. "And now she's coming all this way to plague me," Jinny thought sourly.

"Aren't you going to change out of those filthy jeans?" Petra asked. "They'll be here any minute."

"They won't," said Jinny. "It'll be hours before they arrive."

"You can't be sure," said Petra. "And what would you feel like if they caught you looking like that?"

Jinny groaned.

"Don't just stand there. Go on and get changed."

Jinny gazed hopelessly at her sister. She couldn't be bothered replying. As if it mattered what she was wearing, when the Wrights had seen her hundreds of times in her usual jeans and sweaters. As if it mattered what the paper chains looked like, or how the parcels were arranged around the tree, or how the Christmas cake was decorated. As if any of it mattered when Shantih was starving.

Jinny slammed the door behind her and went through to the kitchen.

"You're not going out?" said her mother.

"I am," said Jinny, and went.

Kelly, who had been lying by the back door, followed at her heels. Jinny had explained to him that he was to stay with her until Ken came back. Kelly had stared at her unblinking, until Jinny had admitted that Ken hadn't mentioned coming back to her, either.

Jinny went down to the ponies' field. "How about a ride?" she suggested, as Bramble came trotting across to her. She caught him by the forelock, manoeuvred him through the gate and led him up to the stables to put his bridle on.

"Now, quietly," she warned, as she sprang on to his back. "If they hear us, they'll stop us."

Cautiously, Jinny circled the ruin of the pottery and turned Bramble towards the moors. He was fresh, not having been ridden since they had broken up four days ago. Jinny let him canter on. "If they call me back now, I can pretend I don't hear them," she thought.

The hills, scoured by the November gales, were bleak under the lead sky. Bramble's hoofs crunched through coral remains of heather. Bracken crackled as they cantered over it, and when Bramble clipped a hidden rock, it rang with a sharper note than the porous summer stone. Kelly loped at their side, a low slung, grey shape.

Since the beginning of December, the Shetlands had been easier to find. The cold weather was drawing them down closer to the farm.

"They'll need hay soon, won't they?" Jinny had said to Mr. MacKenzie, hoping that this would be a sufficiently roundabout approach. What she really wanted to tell him was that he must feed the ponies, for that was the only way Shantih could be fed. Jinny had tried taking a bucket of nuts and oats up to her on the moors, but it had caused such a stramash of biting and kicking that Jinny wasn't keen to try again.

"They wouldn't be looking to it. I've seen the deep snow and they'd rather go scratching for a bite of grass than touch the hay I'd put out for them."

"But Shantih won't be able to do that."

"Then she'd best be learning," Mr. MacKenzie had said.

Jinny found the Shetlands sheltering, rumps to the wind, in the lee of a hill. They watched Bramble's approach, but didn't move. Only the Arab started away in a few panic-swift strides, then turned to watch.

Jinny halted Bramble. She knew if she went any closer, Shantih would gallop off and the whole herd would be disturbed. Looking at the Shetlands, Jinny couldn't tell what condition they were in. Their dense coats and haystack manes and tails made them appear rounded and fat. But Shantih had no camouflage. Jinny could see only too clearly her bones angling through the harsh, staring coat, her sunken quarters and concave neck; even her face seemed chiselled and hollowed where the skin clung tightly to her bones.

"And if she would only come with me," Jinny grieved, "there's a stable and a bed and food, all waiting for her. If she would only trust me."

"Shantih, come with me," she said aloud. "Come on the horse. Come with me." But the icy wind whipped the words from her lips and dried the tears in her eyes.

Jinny waited with Bramble until he had finished his pony nuts, then she put him back out in the field. She had seen the Wrights' car in the drive, so she knew that they had arrived. As she walked towards the house, Jinny could see into the lighted rooms. Mrs. Wright and her mother were in the kitchen, her father and Mr. Wright were drinking beer, while Petra and Susan sat next to each other on the settee, still being stiff and polite. Belinda, in frilled, pink-checked denim, was sitting in the chair that Ken had occupied the night before he left.

"Oh no, no," thought Jinny, "I can't go in there. I can't bear sitting listening to her." And for a moment she almost turned and fled back over the moors to Shantih. But it was only for a moment. Dragged by hooks, like the men in the Old Testament, Jinny went on up the path and into the house.

After dinner, Petra, Mike, Susan and Belinda played Scrabble. Jinny, relieved that only four could play, said that she didn't want a turn.

"She can't spell anyway, can you?" said Belinda.

"She can now," said Mike. "Mr. Gorman makes you be able to spell."

Surprised, Jinny supposed it was true, but the thought of school only made her feel blacker than ever. She sat leafing though a magazine that the Wrights had brought with them, reading about a children's art competition and half listening in to the adults' chat as they talked about Stopton.

"Saw that boy the other day," said Mr. Wright. He was a social worker and knew many of the people that Mr. Manders had worked with. "The boy you had staying down here with you. What was his name again?"

Jinny froze into attention, her eyes still on the magazine in case any of the adults should notice that she was listening.

"Ken," said Mr. Manders. "Ken Dawson."

"That's the one. He's back with his old crowd. Tried to speak to him, but he just looked straight through me. It's when you find a boy like that – good background, everything going for him – who deliberately chooses that kind of company, you wonder sometimes whether it's worth it."

"He left us on an impulse. Up and off," said Mr. Manders. "No explanation."

"Only a matter of time until he's back in the courts. I don't understand that type of boy. I do not understand him."

"If you don't understand him," Jinny thought, "how can you help him?" She hadn't told anyone about Ken's letter, but it looked as if her guess had been correct. Ken was back in Stopton.

Once, Jinny had seen Ken with some of his friends. She knew the way he could look through you. He had been with three other boys and two girls. Their hair, their clothes, and the way they moved, let you know straight away what they thought of the Saturday afternoon shoppers who prowled the streets, grabbing with greedy eyes through shop windows. In Jinny's world, she could be more or less certain about people using handkerchiefs, not crying or shouting in public, not suddenly kissing or attacking each other, but Ken's friends had looked as if they knew nothing about such limitations. They would do what they wanted to do.

"Yet if I had to choose, I'd rather be with them than here with Susan and Belinda," Jinny thought. But it wasn't true. Not deep down true. For one of the boys had looked at Jinny with empty, glittering eyes. She had felt her flesh creep tighter on her bones and had scurried after her mother and Petra, glad to stay close beside them while they shopped, and afterwards, when she had been out in Stopton by herself, she had glanced quickly over her shoulder just in case the boy should be watching her.

"When there's bad in them, it seems as if it has to come out regardless of anything you do for them." But Jinny had lost interest in Mr. Wright's self-satisfaction.

She went up to her room, threw the magazine on a chair and stared out over the moors, into the cold and dark to where Shantih was, wondering what could have been in the letter to make Ken leave them all. Kelly came padding upstairs, pushed open Jinny's door, and lay down at her feet.

"I'm not like Mr. Wright," Jinny told him. "I understand how there are some things that you have to do, no matter what. But what was it, Kelly? Did he tell you?"

"Are you coming down for a cup of coffee?" called Mrs. Manders.

Jinny came back to herself with a start. "No," she shouted, feeling her body stiff with standing for so long at the window.

"We're having hot mince pies."

"Oh," said Jinny and went downstairs.

Christmas was presents – and Belinda crying because her father had bought her the wrong kind of watch; so much food that they all felt sick and cross; and making sure that Belinda wasn't bored.

"She's your guest," her mother kept telling Jinny.

90

"And I am trying," Jinny kept telling her mother. "Everything I can think of I've tried. I'm not interested in Stopton and she's not interested in here. So what can I do?"

"You know she's scared of horses. Why you had to sit her on Punch and take her over the hills to stare at that wretched Arab, I can't imagine. No wonder she was sick," said Petra.

"We only walked. I have to go and see Shantih," retorted Jinny. "You keep telling me to look after her, so I took her with me," she added, ducking away from their criticisms.

The thought of Shantih was like toothache – toothache at the North Pole where there were no dentists. Every day, Shantih seemed to be poorer than she had been the day before. Jinny had tried to get food to her again, but the Arab had refused to come near her, and the Shetlands, in a kicking, squealing mob, had knocked the bucket out of Jinny's hand and gobbled down the oats.

"We're all going for a drive, taking a picnic with us," Mrs. Manders announced brightly after breakfast.

"I'm not," said Jinny.

"Nor me," said Mike.

"You are disgusting children," despaired their mother. "Why can't you come with us?"

"There's only three days left before we go back to school," said Mike, "and I promised Alec that I'd go and see him one day in the holidays."

"You know I hate sitting in a car when I don't need to," said Jinny.

When they had gone, Jinny went to see Shantih. She found her easily, but it was too cold to wait for long and Jinny was glad to ride back down, out of the icy, searing wind. Glad in a way to escape from Shantih, for it wasn't her imagination, as Petra insisted – the flesh really was melting away from Shantih's bones. Jinny could make out each separate rib, and the horse's spine was like a knotted rope linking her flat shoulders to her angular quarters. Jinny could do nothing to help her. Her family didn't believe her – they all said that Mr. MacKenzie knew more about looking after horses than Jinny did, and that she was exaggerating when she said Shantih was starving.

Finmory House was hollow with only Jinny in it, full of sudden creaks and groans that you only noticed when you were alone. Jinny made herself a mug of coffee and cut herself a proper piece of Christmas cake – not a little finger slice that you couldn't taste. She carried them up to her bedroom. The Wrights' magazine was still lying on the chair, and Jinny remembered the art competition. She read about it as she ate her cake.

Sixty pounds was the first prize. It might be enough to pay someone who knew how to train horses to come to Finmory and help her to catch Shantih. Jinny munched marzipan and walked down the hillside towards Finmory. Walking beside her was the man who knew all about horses. He was leading Shantih. "Yes, I expect you'll be able to ride her in a week or two," he said.

The competition was for any kind of picture to represent Wildlife Awareness Year; any medium you liked – collage, watercolour, pastel, oils, anything. Jinny's eyes darted over the rules and regulations.

"I'll paint Shantih," she thought. "Sixty pounds."

She filled a jam jar with water, laid out paper and her box of watercolours on the bedroom floor and sat back on her heels, staring at the white, empty sheet, waiting until her picture grew inside her head, behind her eyes, waiting until she saw it in colour. Then she stretched out her hand, feeling almost blindly for the brush, and began to paint.

When the picture was finished Jinny stood up, hardly glancing at it. She went down to the kitchen, cut another large chunk of cake, and took Kelly for a quick run down to the beach. When she got back, she went slowly upstairs to see if she had managed it.

It was good. She had mirrored the magic, enchanted quality of the Arab, the moment before she turned and fled. Her chestnut coat echoed the russet tones of the bracken that reached away to the mountains and the luminous clarity of the autumn sky.

But it wasn't enough, it needed something more.

"The insects! The drawings I did in the summer."

Jinny felt like a blown-up balloon as she scrabbled

through her drawings to find them. She knew exactly how she was going to do it. With a fine, black, felt-tipped pen, she began to copy the insects on to the foreground of her watercolour.

The black line flowed sure and precise, as all the creeping, crawling things that Jinny had drawn in the summer came to life again on her painting. When she had drawn the insects she didn't stop. She went on to draw sheep, rabbits, foxes, crows, gulls and kestrels, seeing them all as clearly as if she were crouching on the moors, watching them. High above Shantih she drew a golden eagle with its wings outspread. Her drawings made a web of textured living with Shantih burning at the centre. It was the best thing she had ever done.

Jinny found cardboard and paper, wrapped her drawing up and bound it in sellotape. Her hands fumbled as she hurried to get it done before her family returned. Her handwriting sprawled over the label. When she had finished she lay flat on the floor, poured out.

The next day, Jinny rode into Glenbost and posted her entry. The day after that, the Wrights went home.

"Two more days and I'll be back in Mr. Gorman's clutches," Jinny thought, as she watched the Wrights settling themselves into their car. "Not tomorrow but the next day I'll be back at school."

"Don't forget to let me know what you decide," Mr. Wright called from the car.

"Will do," answered Mr. Manders.

"What have you to decide?" Jinny asked, when the Wrights had driven away.

"What's the matter?" said Petra. "Are you going to get a divorce?" It made Jinny wonder what it would be like to be part of a family who couldn't make that sort of joke in case it was true.

"Well, it's like this," began Mr. Manders when they were all inside again, "they still haven't filled my post in Stopton. They've had one bloke in it, but he only lasted a couple of months. They've shuffled things around a bit and they've offered me a promotion. Bill Wright was genned up to persuade me."

"Leave here?" gasped Jinny.

"You mean go back to Stopton?" said Mike.

"But we live here now. This is where we live," said Jinny. "Of course we can't go back. Finmory is home."

"Listen for a minute," insisted Mr. Manders. "It's not as simple as that. There's the cash to consider. I had to pay back all the pot money and that's pretty well all I've made since we've been here. The money from Mum's house won't last for ever. And this chance won't come again."

"What about your book?" asked Petra.

"When, and *if*, it is ever published, I might make two or three hundred pounds – which might feed us for a week or two."

"Once it's spring we can all live on vegetables, like Ken. All you need to buy are the seeds."

"It'll help," said Mr. Manders. "But it's the whole thing of staying here or going back to Stopton. It's now or never. We've got to decide."

Jinny tried to think what it would be like to live in a city again, to walk out of the house on to pavements, to have thousands of people pressing down on you, to go to the pictures and museums again – but she couldn't remember it properly. It had been before Shantih.

"Well, I'm not going back to Stopton," she announced. "I'm for never."

"And you don't need to tell us why," said Petra.

"Mike?" asked Mr. Manders.

"Not likely."

They waited for Petra to give her considered opinion.

"I don't want to change schools again," she said. "I'd feel a bit silly going back when I only left a few months ago."

"There you are. I told you so," said Mrs. Manders to her husband. "Nobody wants to leave. So stop going on at yourself. WE ALL LIKE IT HERE. Ken's done marvels with the garden, and you'll soon get the pottery going again."

"Pity Ken got itchy feet. We need him. Still, that's it settled? No one for Stopton?"

"Of course not," said Jinny.

By the afternoon, when Jinny rode over the moors to

pay her usual visit to Shantih, the sky was heavy with black clouds that had come sweeping in from the sea, greedily engulfing the whole sky. Jinny shuddered and hurried Bramble on. She had never felt the moors so menacing before – even when she had ridden over them at night there hadn't been this sense of waiting, this threat of forces about to be unleashed.

She rode for an hour, searching all the places where the ponies were usually to be found, but there was no sign of them. A wind whistled through the dead bracken and honed the edges of rocks. It seemed to Jinny that there was nothing alive in the whole stretching moorland except herself and Bramble. No birds or rabbits, only a solitary gull that sheered inland, white against the black sky, and cried a warning to her.

Suddenly Jinny turned for home. One second she was searching for the ponies, the next she was cantering back to the safety of Finmory. Nothing was so important as to get off the moors before it was too late.

Lying in bed that night, Jinny counted the bad things – Mr. Gorman and going back to school, the fact that her father had thought about returning to Stopton – and although no one had wanted to go, Jinny knew only too well that once a thing had been talked about that made it possible. Ken being back in Stopton, back with that boy who had looked at Jinny as if he could kill her and hardly notice it, and, worst of all, she had run away from Shantih, had fled home when Shantih might have been needing her. Everyone was predicting snow, and Jinny couldn't imagine how Shantih would manage out on the moors if it came. "There's only me to love her, and I didn't go on looking for her," Jinny thought, and turned away from herself into sleep.

Next morning the clouds hung sulphur and purple, the moors, hills and sea, etched in shades of grey, waited, holding their breath.

Despite the weather, Mrs. Manders organized her three children into Inverburgh for hair cutting and school clothes. Although her shoulder was perfectly better and she had taken the strapping off weeks ago, Jinny had to go into the hospital to let them have a look at it. It was after three when they left Inverburgh, and already the street lights were on. When they branched off for Glenbost, they drove into an opaque, grey darkness.

"Nip out for the milk, someone," Mrs. Manders said, stopping the car at the MacKenzie's farm.

Jinny nipped. "Don't wait for me. I'll walk," she said, glad to escape from the prison of the car.

"Well, take the torch," said her mother, handing out the flashlight that was kept in the glove compartment.

Jinny walked across the yard, feeling that there was something different, and realised that it was the sound of sheep. She could smell them, too, cloying and warm.

"Where have the sheep come from?" Jinny asked Mr. MacKenzie, as he ladled milk into her can.

"Brought them down from the hills," he said. "It's the day we've had of it, but that's them all safe. Not often the weather's for giving us a warning like this."

"You really think it is going to snow?"

"Last time it held off for a day or two, like this, the snow was so deep you couldn't see a wall for it, just flat white snow."

"What about the ponies? Did you bring them down, too?"

"Didn't need bringing. They're all down at the wall behind the barn. Know better than we do what the weather's going to be."

Jinny left the full milk can at the farmhouse door. She ran round to the back of the barn, her feet following the beam of torchlight.

"Shantih," she called. "Shantih."

The torch beam shone through the dense gloom, and she saw the Shetlands crowded together by the wall. The light glinted on eyeballs and showed bushy manes and hairy bodies.

"Shantih," Jinny called again, as she swung the torch beam back and forward, searching the darkness for the Arab. But there was only the Shetlands.

She climbed over the wall and stumbled through the mud, her torch beam cutting wildly through the dark. But there was no panic of startled hoofs, no chestnut shape standing apart from the others. Shantih wasn't there.

Jinny ran back and banged on the farmhouse door.

"Shantih's not with them," she cried, when Mr. Mac-Kenzie, his boots in his hand, a horny toenail sticking through a hole in his sock, opened the door. "She's not there."

"Now that'll be right," he said. "I didn't see her myself."

"Then we'll need to go and find her."

"You take the milk and be off home with you. If she's fool enough to stay out on those hills tonight it's not myself will be bothering with her."

And Mr. MacKenzie slammed the door shut in Jinny's face.

CHAPTER ELEVEN

Jinny's bedroom door creaked as she turned the handle, shattering the silence of the sleeping house. She froze, cradling the door still, hardly breathing as she waited, dreading to hear the sound of someone getting up to investigate the noise. But there was no movement. No one had heard her.

Jinny eased the door open, inch by inch, and slipped out. Cautiously she crept downstairs, testing each step before she put her weight on it. She stood in the hall, waiting for her heart to stop banging so loudly, before she opened the kitchen door. She saw her oilskins hanging from the hallstand, thought that if it did start to snow while she was on the moors they would keep her dry, and reached up for them. A walking stick clattered to the floor. The crash reverberated through the house.

"Run for it. Get out now or they'll stop you," screamed a voice in Jinny's head, but she couldn't make her legs move. No matter how hard she tried, they wouldn't move.

"What are you doing now?" demanded her father from the top of the stairs. He came down two at a time, pulling on his dressing-gown. "Well?"

"I'm going to find Shantih."

"You most certainly are not."

"But I *must* go. Why isn't she with the Shetlands? She must have hurt herself. I've got to find her before it starts snowing. She'll die if I don't find her."

"Now listen to me, Jinny. You know perfectly well that it is quite out of the question for anyone to think of going out there tonight. You know how dangerous it is."

"But Shantih's . . ."

"If you got caught in a blizzard you wouldn't stand a chance, and you know that as well as I do, don't you?"

"Yes, but if I go now I'll be back before the snow. I must go. Anyway, it may not snow."

"You are to do no such thing. I wouldn't let you go this evening and I certainly won't let you go now."

"I've got to . . ."

"Oh, for goodness' sake have some sense. She's probably with the Shetlands by now."

"Then let's go and see," said Jinny. "Please."

"You are going straight back to bed, but before you go, I want your promise that you won't try to go out again tonight."

"I can't . . ."

"Then I'll wake Petra and put up the camp bed in your room for her."

"You wouldn't!"

"I would. Now no more of this nonsense. Promise."

Jinny stared down at the floor. She had to find Shantih. She had to.

"Then I'll wake Petra."

"Oh, all right then. I promise. But when we find Shantih's skeleton on the moors it will be all your fault." And Jinny pushed past her father and ran back to her room. She buried her face in her pillow and cried herself to sleep.

Jinny woke from suffocating nightmares – sharply awake into a moment of not knowing who or what, where or when, only aware of an atmosphere of terror that was everywhere. Then she remembered – Shantih. Jinny sat up. Her alarm clock said half-past six. It was morning.

"Promise you won't try to go out there again tonight," demanded her father's voice.

"But it's morning now," Jinny thought. "I only promised that I wouldn't go out at night."

She got up and dressed. Hesitated in front of her bedroom door. If they caught her again she wouldn't have another chance. She gritted her teeth, knowing what she had to do. "Just do it. Don't think. Do it."

She walked across her bedroom to the window that looked out on to the hills and opened it. The darkness was a solid wall, the cold swept in at her, but it still wasn't snowing.

"If I don't go, Shantih will die. If I don't go, Shantih will die." Jinny repeated the words under her breath until they made a stronger pattern than her fear. "If I don't go, Shantih will die."

She sat astride the windowsill, reached to her left and felt the rusty drainpipe. Before their mother had caught him, Mike had climbed up and down the drainpipe. Up once to rescue a kitten and down once for a dare. Jinny had watched him with the scared fascination of someone who has no head for heights.

"If I don't go, Shantih will die."

Jinny stretched out with both hands and brought her other leg over the windowsill. She crouched there for a second, then squirmed her weight on to the pipe. For a terrifying moment she felt it move away from the wall, and thought she was going to be too heavy for it. She clung tightly – knees, feet, and hands, her cheek pressed against the stone. "If I don't go, Shantih will die." The icy metal gnawed at her hands, froze her body as she slithered down. Halfway down, the pipe branched out, and she was able to rest her feet before she went on. "If I don't go, Shantih will die." But her arms and legs were limp, and buckled under her weight. She couldn't make them hold on, knew that she must fall, but in the blackness she had no idea how far away the ground was. Her feet slipped away from the pipe. She hung for a moment by her hands, but they wouldn't hold her and she fell.

A rhododendron bush caught her. She struggled out of it, tested her arms and legs to make sure they were still attached to her, then realised that she had made it. "Pretty good, pretty good," she praised herself.

Jinny walked through the dark to the stable and felt along the inside of the door until she found a halter. She stumbled her way to a bin, then filled her anorak pockets with oats. Her foot kicked something that had been standing on the floor. It fell over, and Jinny crouched down to find out what it was. Her fingers closed on the torch. She must have left it there last night after she had fed the ponies. "That's a sign," she thought, switching it on gratefully. "Now I'm bound to find her."

An old pair of Petra's wellingtons were standing in a corner. They were a bit big, but had heavy socks rolled up inside them. "Better than my sandshoes," Jinny decided, and put them on. She found an ancient sweater of oiled wool that belonged to her father and pulled it on over her anorak, tying it round the waist with a handy piece of binder twine. She shone the torch through to the other half of the stable. The thick bed of straw, which Jinny had kept fresh for weeks, waited for Shantih.

"I'll find her, and this time I'll bring her home," Jinny swore as she left the shelter of the stable and set out into the dark.

First she checked the farm, just in case Shantih had joined the others, but there were still only the uneasy flock of sheep and the Shetlands.

"All right for you," Jinny told them. "Why didn't you wait for Shantih? Little hairy pigs to come running down here and leave her up there alone."

Jinny followed the farm track that led out on to the moors. She stomped her feet down into the rutted mud, clapped her hands, pulled the polo neck of the sweater over her head and shouted the Arab's name into the blanket dark. A burn crossed the track and Jinny turned to follow it up over the moors. She knew it would take her close to where they had picnicked the day the circus van crashed. She hoped from that vantage point she would be able to spot Shantih. Jinny felt sure that something must have happened to her, that she needed help.

Jinny tried to keep the stream on her right, but often the marshy ground made her take wide detours. If she tried to hurry, it only made her stumble and fall more than ever. Her feet caught on clumps of reeds and heather roots.

Once she dropped the torch. It went out as it hit the ground and the blackness sighed in. Jinny dropped to her knees, felt around herself in a wide circle. "Don't move your feet or you'll never find it," she thought as she searched over the ground. There was a clatter as the torch rolled over – its light came back on, and Jinny clutched it to her. Tripping and falling, she trudged on, always listening for any sound that might be Shantih. Her torch beam swathed through the dark. "Shantih!"

Gradually the darkness grew less dense, a long luminous streak shone in the east, and a grey light moved across the sky, revealing waves of petrified moorland lifeless as a moonscape. Jinny peered into the greyness, searching everywhere for the chestnut glint of Shantih, but she could see no sign of her. Jinny meant to climb to the top of the hillside, then quarter back towards Finmory. She tried to run, swinging the halter rope, shouting songs at the top of her voice, hoping that the disturbance might rouse Shantih, but in the vast reaches of the moor Jinny's voice was no more than a shrill squeaking. The mountains and the moors were indrawn and fortified. Any life that was still abroad was no concern of theirs as they meditated on the coming snow.

The first flake splodged down on to Jinny's arm and lay on the black sweater like a soft fifty-pence piece. Another fell on her face, hot against her numb cheek. Jinny looked up and saw the snow coming hurtling down, not floating filigree, but a silent bombardment that beat down faster and faster – came pelting, hurtling straight at her. Jinny bent her head and ploughed on.

In no time, the hillside was patchworked grey and white. When Jinny stopped and looked round again, the white was a smooth covering, only broken here and there by dark patches sheltered from the snowfall by overhanging rocks.

"I must go on," Jinny hold herself. "When I reach the top, I'll easily spot Shantih against the white."

Yet when she stopped again and looked back, she realised with a shock that she could hardly see for any distance. The falling snow was thicker than fog. The sound of her own breathing was loud in its silence.

"I'll need to go back or I'll be lost. If I go on now, I won't be able to find my way home. But I can't go back without Shantih."

Jinny switched on the torch again. Its beam bounced back from the falling snow as if it were a solid wall. "Dark as night," Jinny thought, and suddenly, as if it had been whispered in her ear, she knew where Shantih would be. If she had hurt herself, and Jinny was sure she had, she would have gone to where she felt safest, where she always went at night, to the standing stones. For a moment Jinny hesitated – to reach the standing stones she would need to strike across the moors. "I should go home," she thought. "I should." Then she spun round, waded through the burn, and set off in the direction of the standing stones, fighting her way through the thick suffocation of the blizzard.

"You are mad," said one voice.

"If I don't find her, she'll die."

"You'll die if you're lost in this," the voice assured her, but Jinny plunged on.

Now that it was snowing, it wasn't so cold. The moors were no longer indrawn and menacing, but almost like spring, making Jinny laugh aloud as she ran, leaping into hollows already smoothed flat with drifting snow. She threw snowballs through the steady curtain of flakes, caught snow on her outstretched tongue and thought about sledging.

"I'm O.K.," she grinned, recognising a twisted rowan tree. "I know that tree. It's not far now. And Shantih will be there at the standing stones waiting for me."

Jinny laughed aloud as she galloped through the snow. In the magic of this world there was nothing to hold on to – no time, no place – so that when she met the rowan tree for a second time, she had to stand and stare suspiciously at it, wondering if she had been away from it or if she had been standing there all the time.

"You've been following me," she shouted at the rowan, but her accusation was muffled by the closeness of the snow. Jinny took two strides away from the tree and it had vanished.

"Well, that's that tree sorted out," Jinny chuntered to herself as she went on lifting her feet slowly up and down, up and down. "I'd have been better in my sandshoes. I might have known that Petra's boots would hold me back."

She sat down in the snow to take off the wellingtons.

"I'll skim over the top of the snow in my bare feet," she thought, but she couldn't manage to pull off the boots. "Need to rest my hands. It's all the parsing that Mr. Gorman makes me do. They're worn out." She spread out her hands, watching the snow bury them in a blanket of white. It was surprisingly warm sitting in the snow. Jinny lay down. She closed her eyes, but the white blizzard was inside her head as well, it raged behind her eyes, furious as the storm-tossed crests of the waves. It became a white horse, wild and untameable.

"Shantih! !" screamed Jinny, and leapt to her feet. She stood shaking her head, swinging her arms against her body, stamping her feet.

Another second and she would have been asleep. They would never have found her. She would have been dead. No more Jinny Manders.

"You've got to keep moving," Jinny told herself. "Keep your mind on real things. You've got to get to the standing stones."

Jinny moved like a robot through the deepening snow. Every six steps she stopped to touch her toes, stretch her arms out to the sides and then above her head. She thought of Shantih, beginning at their visit to the circus, and went over every single time she had seen the Arab. Then she went on into the future, thinking of when she would be able to school her and ride her – then she repeated all she had ever read about schooling horses.

Something sitting on the high crags whistled for a wind. Jinny heard it coming, moaning over the moor, roaring over the hills until it reached her, engulfing her in white spirals as it plucked up the newly fallen flakes to dance them in mad whirlwinds that mingled with the falling snow.

The voice of the wind whispered and called, making Jinny shout to it, thinking that someone was there. She began to see figures in the blown eddies. She ran to them, thinking it was Shantih, but before she could reach them the wind sucked them away, and there was only the steady, endless fall of snow.

Jinny was crying now. She was cold again. Her teeth wouldn't stop chattering. And she was afraid. Sometimes the wind-blown shapes were monstrous and evil, sometimes tiny darting things that came chittering, whispering, pecking at Jinny with iron teeth, but were gone before she could catch them.

Jinny still called the Arab as she staggered blindly on, but now she was calling to Shantih to come and save her, to plunge through the terrors, scattering them to nothing with her real presence.

Jinny stopped suddenly, stood perfectly still, every sense skinned. She was sure she had heard a voice calling her name. It had been quite different to the moaning chatter of the wind, as real as her mother's voice waking her from a nightmare. She heard it again.

"I'm here. I'm here," she yelled. "Here I am!"

A snow shape loomed towards her. Was real. Was Ken.

"How you doin' then?" he asked.

"Ken!" screamed Jinny, and fell through the snow into his arms.

"Go easy now," he said, comforting her. "What you doing up here?"

"I'm looking for Shantih."

"That's what we reckoned. Saw a sheltered bit in the rocks back there. Come on."

Jinny and Ken went back and crawled into an overhang between two rocks. It stank of sheep, but was dark and gentle after the glaring whiteness.

"Call me Bernard," said Ken, taking a bottle filled with brandy from an inside pocket of his parka. He handed it to Jinny. "Two gulps, that's all. Don't want to have to carry you home."

Jinny gulped and spluttered, then felt the heat of the brandy flow through her. She couldn't stop shaking. "When did you come back?"

"This morning."

"Are you going to stay?"

Ken grinned. "Typical woman. Yes, I'm staying. It was too much. They don't want to hear what I could tell them. So. Here, have some food." And Ken produced chocolate, nuts and raisins from the depths of his pockets.

104

"Now," he said, when Jinny had eaten, "let's get back. The others are out looking for you."

"Back? Oh no. I'm going to the standing stones. That's where Shantih is."

Ken looked straight at her, considering.

"She'll die if we don't find her. How would you like it if people stopped looking for you? Just went home and left you to die?"

"How do you know she's there?"

"I know," said Jinny.

"Well, have another slug of brandy before we go."

When they squeezed back out on to the moor, the snow had almost stopped. The flakes hung in the air, drifted gently down from a clear sky. A miraculous white world stretched about them, rolling, curved, deceptively gentle.

"Whee!" exulted Ken.

"Come on," said Jinny, as she turned towards the shards of stone, dark against the sky, and began to plod doggedly towards them.

"Go lightly," said Ken. "Let your breath take you. Unhook your mind and we're there already."

As they reached the final climb to the standing stones, Ken slowed down, letting Jinny battle on ahead. He understood that she had to be the first to reach Shantih, or have time to hold on to herself if her intuition was wrong and the Arab wasn't there.

Snow rose like a smoke screen in front of Jinny as she floundered through it. Her eyes were fixed on the upright slabs of stone, their gaunt outlines softened by the snow – but she could see no sign of Shantih. The snow around the stones was as undisturbed, as pristine, as the rest of the moor.

Jinny had stopped calling the Arab. If she wasn't at the standing stones, Jinny didn't know what she would do next. Ken might make her go home. Both her father and Mr. MacKenzie were out on the hills searching for her. It would be bad enough listening to what they would have to say to her if she found Shantih, but much, much worse if she had to go back without finding her.

A few yards away from the stones, Jinny stopped.

105

"But she must be here. She must . . . Shantih," Jinny yelled as she dashed forward. "Shantih!"

In the circle of the stones Jinny stood desolate, staring hopelessly about her. Shantih wasn't there.

"Please God. Please."

She ran desperately through the circle to the far side, where the snow had drifted smooth and high – a white, lifeless emptiness.

But there was something different about one of the drifts. It was somehow the wrong shape.

Jinny fell on her knees and dug into the snow with her hands and arms, scattering it furiously about, shouting to Ken to come and help as she cleared the snow away from the outstretched body of the Arab.

CHAPTER TWELVE

"She's dead, isn't she," Jinny said, not really asking, because she didn't need Ken to tell her what she could see for herself.

"Looks like," agreed Ken.

"I'm too late. If I'd gone straight from the farm last night . . ."

"No good saying 'if'. Does no good."

Suddenly Shantih kicked back with a hind leg, a violent reflex action.

"She's not!" screamed Jinny. "She's alive!"

The mare's eye opened slowly, stared vacantly, then focussed. Seeing humans, she swung her head up, trying to escape from them. She struggled to stand, but her legs slipped away from her in the snow and she fell back, her tongue hanging loosely from the side of her mouth.

"We've got to make her stand up," said Jinny. She knelt beside the Arab, talking love to her as she slipped the halter around her head and knotted it securely. "Come on Shantih. Up, get up. You can't stay here. You're safe now. We've found you but you mustn't give in. You've got to try. We must get you back home."

Jinny ran her hands over the thin neck and shoulder and

pulled Shantih's ears between her hands, remembering from somewhere that this was the way to warm a cold horse.

"I'm touching her," Jinny thought. "I'm really with her for the first time," and joy, stronger than any brandy flowed through her, warming her, giving her strength to go on fighting.

Again Shantih stretched out her neck and head and struggled to lift herself with her forelegs.

"Don't let her stop," warned Ken. He was at her shoulder, pushing with all his strength to stop the mare sliding back down. Jinny stood at Shantih's head, pulling on the halter.

"Get up! Get up!" she yelled, but Shantih's hoofs splayed out and she collapsed again.

"Let her rest a minute," said Ken. He took off his parka and spread it under Shantih's forelegs. "Give her some grip. Right, now try her. We've got to get her moving before the snow starts again."

Jinny glanced at the sky. The bright clearness was clouding over – burgeoning, purple-black clouds jostled and swelled.

"O.K.," Jinny tugged at the halter rope. "Get up," she yelled. "Get up with you."

Shantih half lifted her head. She looked as old and worn as the most weary of Stopton's cart ponies. Her eyes were dull and glazed, and her long, scraggy neck gave her a weird, haunting look. Despite Jinny's efforts, she sank back into the snow.

"Here, give me the rope," said Ken. "Now, when I get her head up, don't give her the chance to pack it in."

"Don't hurt her," said Jinny. "She isn't strong enough to stand."

"If we can't get her up, we'll have to leave her. Tom's out searching for you, and Mr. MacKenzie. If we all get caught on these hills tonight it won't do any of us much good."

"But you wouldn't leave her here?"

"Yes I would. Rather one animal than four humans. Now."

Ken jerked savagely at the rope, jerked life into Shantih.

He raged and lashed at her with his voice, forced her to keep on struggling. Jinny rattled her fists on the mare's bony sides, kicked against the deadness of her quarters, ran back and launched herself against the stubborn bulk.

Shantih dug her forehooves against Ken's parka. For a terrifying moment she stayed balanced between standing and falling back. Then, with a whinny of pain, she was upright.

"Very good," praised Ken. "Well done."

"Look at her leg," cried Jinny. "That's why she was stranded up here."

Shantih's near hind leg was swollen from the fetlock to above the hock. It stuck out stiffly behind her, looking as if someone had stuffed a feather cushion beneath the skin. Jinny ran her hand over the swelling and felt it burning hot. Shantih flinched away from her and nearly fell.

"Get her home first," said Ken, and Jinny saw him glance quickly at the sky. The clouds leaned over the hills and the remaining patch of clear sky shrank as they watched it.

"Right," agreed Jinny, taking the halter from Ken. "See the burn down there? We go down to it and then follow it along. There's a track through the bracken after that, but we'll just need to guess. Perhaps we'll be able to see Finmory by then."

They made slow progress, black specks crawling over a white wilderness. At every step they had to stop and wait, while Shantih balanced herself on her three sound legs and dragged her swollen leg behind her.

"Keep her moving," ordered Ken.

"She wants to rest," pleaded Jinny.

"She can't. Don't let her stop."

Ken walked ahead of them, checking their way for unsuspected drifts, sudden pits, treacherous boulders hidden in the snow, or bogs, their warning green lost under the white.

They reached the foot of the slope and started to follow the burn. All the sky was black cloud now, and the hills had slipped out of sight into grey gloom. Every now and again a solitary snowflake floated down, making them look up anxiously, expecting to see the sky falling about them.

Jinny, stumbling at Shantih's side, hardly knew where she was. Sometimes she thought she was alone again, that she had found Shantih by herself, then Ken, shouting a warning, would bring her back to reality and she would answer him, saying nothing – only wanting to make sure that he was really there.

"We haven't far to go now. There's a warm bed, and hay, and a feed," Jinny told the mare, trying not to look at the bony face, not to hear Shantih's harsh breathing, not to see the grossly swollen leg. "When we get back we'll phone for the vet. He'll come at once. You'll be all right then."

"It's about here that we leave the burn," Jinny called. "Finmory is over that way."

"Certain?"

"Think so."

"Right. Don't let her stop."

Now they had left the stream behind them, the white landscape was all the same. They couldn't pick out any familiar features. Everything was transformed by the snow.

"We should be further down," Ken said, stopping to peer about him. "We're wrong. We want to go further this way."

Jinny followed, with Shantih dragging and stumbling at her side.

When the snow began to fall they stopped again.

"Watch out," Ken warned – but it was too late. Shantih was down. Jinny looked helplessly at her, watching the snow flakes settle on her chestnut coat. She hadn't the energy left to force her up again.

Suddenly they heard voices. Listened for a second.

"Tom!" yelled Ken. "Tom! Over here!"

"Dad," cried Jinny, as she plunged towards the sound. "I've found Shantih. I've found her."

Mr. MacKenzie and Mr. Manders strode towards them.

"Thank God," said Mr. Manders. "You blasted idiot of a child."

"I'd tan the hide off you if you were mine," added Mr. MacKenzie. "What were you after having us all out on the hill on a day like this?"

"It's her leg," said Jinny. "I think it's poisoned."

"That wastrel of a mare," muttered Mr. MacKenzie, as Jinny hurried him over to look at Shantih's leg.

"Man, am I glad to see you. We're spaced out," said Ken.

Mr. MacKenzie took Shantih's halter rope and swung it at the mare, hitting her about the head and neck.

"Don't hurt her," cried Jinny, but Shantih had already splattered to her feet.

"She's no lap dog. It's a horse you're dealing with. Aye, it's the poisoned leg, and a real bad one at that," Mr. MacKenzie said, examining Shantih. "Poor brute. Well, let's be getting her back. Finmory's nearest. Have you the stall for her?"

"It's been ready for weeks," said Jinny.

"Then we'll be getting her there as fast as you like." And the farmer set off confidently into the gloom.

"How can you tell where we are?" demanded Mr. Manders.

"I'll be sixty-seven next July, if the Lord allows, and I've been on these hills since I could walk. It would be the sorry day if the wee touch of snow were to make me lose my way."

As they followed Mr. MacKenzie, the snow grew heavier. Jinny was longing to be home, to be warm and safe again, to be inside, out of the snow.

"You'll need to phone the vet at once," she said to her father.

He brushed snow out of his beard and looked down at her sternly.

"Will do, whenever we get home. I'll say no more just now, but when this is over you and I are going to have a very serious talk."

Jinny nodded, a lump choking in her throat at her father's words. "How can you do it?" she thought. "How can you balance not hurting people, not worrying people and doing the things you have to do?" – but it was too impossible to think about now.

When they reached Finmory, Jinny led Shantih into the box she had prepared for her and took off her halter. The mare fell heavily into the straw, her injured leg uppermost. She stretched out with a groan, her head sank down, and

110

she lay still. Tears poured down Jinny's face. She had imagined this moment so often, bringing Shantih home to Finmory, but never had she pictured it like this.

"Can't get through," said Mr. Manders, coming back from the phone.

"Aye," said Mr. MacKenzie. "The Ardtallon line'll be down, but I doubt if Jim would be coming out on a night like this. Even if he'd the mind to it he wouldn't be getting here. A pity for the mare. It's a wonder the new drugs they have these days. Might have pulled her through."

Jinny scrubbed her face against the sleeve of her sweater, pushed her hair back from her face and straightened her shoulders. A moment ago she had been longing to be in the house, drinking hot soup, telling the others about her adventure before she went to bed. The thought of sleep, of being able to let her eyes close, had filled her mind, but now she pushed the temptation away. She hadn't fought all day to bring Shantih home just to let her die now.

"Well, what shall we do?" Jinny demanded. "If the vet can't come we'll need to look after her ourselves."

"Aye, but you don't give up easy," said Mr. MacKenzie. "You'll not be having a horse rug?"

"No, but there's plenty on my bed."

"No need, I'll go and get you one. Take a wisp over her and try to warm her up a bit."

Jinny twisted a wisp out of straw and knelt beside Shantih, rubbing her over with strong sweeps of her arm. The mare was nothing but bone under her tight skin. Jinny straightened her forelock and ran her hands tenderly over Shantih's face.

"You're all right now," she murmured. "You're safe now. I'll stay with you until you're better."

Mr. MacKenzie came back with a heavy horse blanket, bandages and a tin of kaolin paste. He threw the blanket over Shantih and packed straw underneath it.

"Now then, let's be seeing to her leg." His gnarled hands felt Shantih's leg. "Aye, it's nasty. Would you look at that. There's the puncture that's caused the damage."

The swelling was hard and tight and burning hot. Jinny could hardly believe that it could be caused by the tiny wound.

"It's got the dirt in it, but we'll put the poultice on and hope for the best, though I'm doubting she's too far gone. The poison's right through her."

Mr. MacKenzie showed Jinny how to heat up the tin of kaolin paste on top of the Aga, carry it out to the stable, spread some on a pad, slap the hot poultice on to Shantih's leg where it was punctured, then bandage it into place.

"You'll need to change it yourself in the morning."

Jinny nodded.

"I'll be away then, and get you to your bed."

"I'm staying up with Shantih."

"Your mother'll be putting the hems on that notion."

"I am."

"Then I dare say you'll be getting your own way as usual. Try her with a drop of water – be taking the chill off it now. I'll come over tomorrow and we'll make a mash if she's still with us. Don't be upsetting yourself now if she dies. She's no but an animal."

"She isn't going to die," stated Jinny.

Her mother insisted that Jinny changed into dry clothes and had a proper meal, but she didn't argue when Jinny said she was going to stay with Shantih.

"She's unconscious," said Petra. "What difference does it make whether you're there or not?"

"I think she knows," said Jinny. "Knows that she's not been abandoned, not just left with no one caring. That there's someone fighting on her side."

It was after midnight when Mr. Manders went out for a last look at Jinny. He expected to find her asleep, and was ready to carry her into the house and up to her bed. He heard the painful rasp of Shantih's breathing as he approached the stable. An oil lamp cast flickering shadows over the cobwebbed walls. Jinny was kneeling by Shantih's head. The soft murmur of her voice stopped as she realised that her father was there.

"How is she?" her father asked.

"She's O.K.," said Jinny fiercely.

Her father waited for a minute or two.

"Sure you won't come to bed?"

"Sure."

112

There was nothing he could do to help her. He shut the stable door and walked slowly back through the snow. "Even your own children," he thought. "You can't live for them. They all have to live for themselves. Go through it all for themselves."

Ken brought flasks of coffee and sandwiches at about four in the morning. He stayed, sitting cross-legged in a corner of the box, until it was light outside, a silent, luminous, white light.

Jinny changed the poultice on Shantih's leg. The swelling was still hard and tight. Several times during the night she had offered the mare water, but she couldn't even get her to lift her head. Jinny had sponged her muzzle and bathed away the matter from her closed eyes, but Shantih had shown no sign of knowing that Jinny was there.

Mr. MacKenzie came over after lunch.

"No dead yet?" he said. "She's no giving in easy. I've brought the bran, but from the look of her she'll not be interested."

"Is there no way we can get the vet to come?" pleaded Jinny.

"You'll not be getting through to Jim until the men have been out to fix the wires, and from the sound of it the forecast is no much good."

"Where does the vet live?" Ken asked.

"A house the other side of Ardtallon. You'd know it by the wee men in the garden, though I'm thinking they'd be under the snow this weather, with their wee red caps pulled down over their ears."

It was after eight when Ken returned from Ardtallon. Although he hadn't said anything, Jinny had guessed that he was going to try and reach the vet. She didn't hear him coming into the stable, but looked up to see him standing there watching her, and she knew from the blankness in his eyes that he'd been unsuccessful.

"He wasn't there," Ken told her. "He was out at a farm when the snow started. Stranded. I told his wife how it is here, so he'll come if he can. She didn't think there was much hope until the snow lifted."

"Thanks for trying," said Jinny, her voice shaky with disappointment. At the back of her mind had been the

113

hope that the vet would come back with Ken. "Thanks for going back out into the snow." Jinny shuddered, remembering the terror of being lost in the white wilderness. It seemed a long time ago. Something she had read about or dreamt. Now the only real thing in her life was to stay with Shantih, to fight with her for the next breath and the next. Not to let her give in. To be there with her.

Ken crouched down beside the Arab. She had been poor before, but now the fever that gripped her had wasted away all the flesh and muscle. Her bones seemed jumbled together, her legs were like the legs of a discarded marionette, chucked down carelessly on the straw.

"She's much worse," said Jinny in a flat, expressionless voice. "And there's nothing I can do to help her. If the vet doesn't get here, she'll die."

"We should know what to do ourselves," Ken said. "Once we would have known what herbs and plants to use to cure a fever, and clean her leg, but now all we can do is wait for someone else." And he thought that he would find out about plants, how they could be used to cure, then the next time something like this happened he would be able to help.

"What's the weather like?"

"In Ardtallon they're all expecting more snow."

Jinny said nothing. More snow would mean there was no hope of the vet getting through tonight.

"How about some kip?"

"No."

Ken left her alone with Shantih, and Jinny settled down again at the Arab's head. She was better alone. Although she had to admit that Shantih didn't show any sign of noticing them, Jinny felt that her family dropping in and chatting disturbed her. And she had to answer them, taking away her concentration from Shantih.

"I couldn't sleep," Jinny told her mother when she came down before midnight to try and persuade Jinny to come in to bed.

"This is the last night, then. Tomorrow morning you must get some sleep. Ken will stay with her."

Jinny thought that she could argue about it tomorrow. Now she only wanted to be left alone.

"You're going to live," Jinny murmured to Shantih. "Soon it will be spring again, and you'll be well and fit. I'll ride you everywhere. We'll go away together for weeks and weeks, riding on every day. I'll pitch my tent somewhere different each night. Sometimes by the sea, and we'll gallop over the sands and swim out into the waves. We'll go to gymkhanas, and you'll win the showing and the jumping. They'll all have heard about you, and when they see us riding into the show field they'll think that I'm only a scruffy trekker, then someone will recognise you. 'That's Shantih,' they'll say. 'Haven't you heard about her?' . . ."

Jinny's voice, whispering into Shantih's ear, made less sound that the mare's irregular breathing; less sound than the scuttering of mice in the rafters; made no disturbance at all beyond the lamp lit globe which contained the girl and the Arab. But Jinny's voice persisted. It went on and on into the night. Defying her sleeping family, defying the remote withdrawal of the white silent world – defying all the common sense that picked at the back of her mind, urging her to sleep, insisting that anything she did could make no difference, telling her not to be so silly. Jinny's voice whispered on.

At first, Jinny didn't notice the pattering, then thought it was only mice. But it was brisk and steady, tapping, drumming, beating – growing stronger each moment. She dashed to the stable door and stared out. It was pouring with rain. Not more snow, but rain. Rain that would clear the roads.

By two in the morning, when Jinny changed Shantih's poultice, it was still pouring. Trees were bare again, their snow blossom vanished. Slabs of snow overhung the eaves of the house, leaving black gaps in the white thatch. The snow on the ground was gnawed and pitted by the steady downpour.

Jim Rae, the vet, reached Finmory shortly after four. Jinny heard his Land-Rover and ran out of the stable to meet him.

"Thank you, oh, thank you for coming," she cried.

"Thank the lad who had my wife so churned up she was turning me on the doorstep to get me here. Well, let's have a look at the horse."

The vet knelt and examined Shantih. Jinny waited, her teeth clenched, afraid to hear what he would have to say. Before he spoke, Jim Rae opened his bag, fitted phials to his syringe, and injected Shantih three times.

"She's still with us," he said, standing up, "and if she'd been for packing it in, she wouldn't be here now. The jabs I've given her should kill the infection, but she's had a long fight of it."

"But she will get better?" demanded Jinny.

"She's very weak," said the vet, "but her heart's strong, and she's fighting. If she can hold out until the drugs take effect, she'll make it. Now how about a cup of tea? Is there only yourself up?"

"I shouldn't leave her."

"Och, come away with you. You'll not be refusing me a cup of tea."

"Oh no, of course not. It's just . . ."

The vet steered Jinny out of the stables. "You've done fine," he told her. "My wife says the place is full of the gossip about yourself setting off in the snow to save her. She'll manage a few minutes by herself. There's no more you can do for her now."

Jim Rae sat down at the kitchen table and lit his pipe, while Jinny struggled to fill the kettle and put it on the Aga. She put the biscuit tin on the table, and it seemed very important that she should get it in exactly the correct spot. Not too close to the vet or he would think that she was trying to make him eat them, not too close to herself or he would think she was being greedy. Jinny stood, stupidly moving the tin backwards and forwards. Then she collapsed into a chair. She laid her head on the table. Her eyes closed.

"When I've made your tea, I must get back to Shantih," she said, but her eyelids wouldn't open. She was asleep.

Ken came downstairs to see if Jinny needed any help, thinking she was heating up the kaolin.

Jim Rae introduced himself. "I'm brewing up. The official brewer has passed out. Would you like a cup?"

"She's bushed," said Ken. "Days since she's had any kip."

"Let her sleep. There's nothing more she can do."

116

"I'll carry her up to bed. Shantih?"

The vet shook his head. "Not good," he said. "But plenty of spirit. I don't often see a horse as far gone as that one and still breathing. She may pull through. It's thanks to the lass, if she does."

CHAPTER THIRTEEN

When Jinny woke up, it was broad daylight. She couldn't think what she was doing in bed when she should have been with Shantih. Pulling on jeans and struggling into her sweater, she pushed her feet into her shoes, and, still half asleep, fumbled her way downstairs. There was no one about.

She ran through the kitchen and out into the yard. It had stopped raining, but the ground was porous and dank. Everywhere there was the sound of water – dripping from trees, swollen burns gushing and frothing down from the moors, the remaining islands of snow shrinking and flowing away. Only the tops of the mountains were still white. Low in the west, the sun made a glistening thumb print through the pearl grey clouds. Jinny realised that it must be late in the afternoon.

She dashed across the yard. At the door of the stable she stopped, afraid to go in. She wrapped her arms round her body, and stood shivering, digging her fingers into her shoulders. If Shantih was worse . . .If she was dead – only a lifeless bulk lying covered in the straw . . . But Jinny had to find out. She had to go on and discover what had happened while she had been asleep.

Jinny took a deep breath. She opened the stable door, waited for a second, surrounded by the familiar bins and sacks and the towering bales of hay. Then she turned her head slowly, not wanting to look, but knowing there was nothing else she could do.

The Arab was standing with her head over the half door of the box, watching her.

For a moment, Jinny could only stand and stare, could hardly allow herself to believe what she saw. Shantih gave a small whinny, flurrying her nostrils, welcoming Jinny.

"You're better!" Jinny cried. "You're better! Oh horse, horse, horse!" And Jinny was opening the box door and flinging her arms around Shantih's neck, pressing her face against the thin neck, clapping the bony shoulder and rubbing her hands over the mare's harsh coat. Shantih turned her head, nuzzling Jinny's shoulder. Her face was still gaunt and wasted, but her dark eyes were calm and bright, her ears pricked and alert.

"And you're not afraid of me any longer. You know me now, know that I'd never hurt you. Oh, Shantih."

Jinny heard a sound at the stable door, she looked up and saw her family and Ken.

"She's better," Jinny shouted to them. "She's not going to die."

"We know," said her father, as they all came crowding round Shantih. "We wanted you to find out for yourself. The vet was here again yesterday. He was pleased with her then and she's come on a bit today."

"Yesterday?" queried Jinny.

"You've been asleep for a day and a night and most of today," said Mike.

"I haven't!" exclaimed Jinny. Maybe she was still asleep. So often had she dreamed of standing like this, Shantih lipping at her outstretched palm, her breath warm and trusting. Jinny pinched herself hard, but she didn't wake up. It was all real, was truly happening.

"Here's the vet now," said Mr. Manders, as they heard the Land-Rover churning its way up the drive. "He said he'd try to come back today."

Jim Rae slammed the Land-Rover door shut and came into the stable with a long, striding walk.

"Well, how's the miracle horse?" he asked. "And her rescuer conscious again. Things are looking up. Unbelievable, really. Some stamina there to pull her through."

When the vet had left and her family had gone back into the house, Jinny filled Shantih's water bucket, mucked out and put down a fresh bed of deep straw. Every few minutes she would stop what she was doing and just stand watching Shantih pull at her hay net. She would go up to the Arab and rub her neck, run Shantih's ears through her

118

hands and talk to her. Jinny's mouth stretched from ear to ear with sheer happiness.

The swelling in Shantih's leg had gone down a lot, and the vet had said that now the poison had been cleared out of her system it was only a question of time, good feeding and care until she was perfectly fit again.

"Soon you'll be quite, quite better," Jinny told Shantih before she left her for the night. "You're really mine now, to stay with me for ever. Soon I'll be able to ride you."

Happiness overflowed in Jinny. She went back to say goodnight to Shantih for one last time, to straighten her silk-fine forelock and make certain that her rug was on correctly. She could hardly bear to leave her.

"And that's not all," said Mike. "School . . ."

"Thought you were keeping it a surprise?" interrupted Mrs. Manders.

"Oh, so I am," remembered Mike.

But Jinny hadn't been paying any attention to him. She was galloping Shantih over the flat sand of Finmory Bay, the sea wind blowing out the mare's mane and tail as her flying hoofs crescented the sand.

"You've missed two days," said Mike, as they rode into Glenbost the next morning.

Jinny had hardly given it a thought. Even now, with Mr. Gorman's power coming closer and closer, she wasn't really thinking about him. She was hoping that Ken would look after Shantih properly.

"I hope he remembers to shake out the hay before he fills her net," Jinny said.

"Who?" said Mike. "Mr. Gorman? More likely to shake you out."

"He won't," said Jinny. "I've got a note." And she couldn't think why Mike was laughing.

They left Bramble and Punch in their field and went across to school.

"Who stuck the snowmen on the windows?" Jinny asked in surprise, looking at the cotton wool figures glued to the glass. It was absolutely the last thing she could imagine Mr. Gorman allowing.

But before Mike had time to answer, the other children, who had been standing in a group in the school doorway, came out to meet them. Dolina was first. Jinny stood still. She felt the familiar clutch of fear tighten her stomach as she remembered the misery of sitting next to Dolina's silent back.

Dolina marched straight up to Jinny. Her cod eyes looked over Jinny's shoulder.

"I'm sorry about last term," she said. "Not speaking. It wasn't your fault that Mr. Gorman wouldn't be listening to you. We'll not be keeping it going this term?"

Jinny's mouth fell open in total amazement, but before she could think of what to say to Dolina, the other children were pushing round her.

"Weren't you afraid to be going up the mountains by yourself and in the storm?"

"How were you knowing that the horse would be at the Stones?"

"My father says there was a man went up there in the snow one winter and they never found him again. Not ever a trace even."

Jinny listened in astonishment. She had been expecting that if they had heard about her adventure on the moor they would only make fun of her.

"Right, children. In you come," called a woman's voice. Standing in the school doorway was a young woman with hair almost as long as Jinny's.

"She's Miss Broughton. The new teacher," explained Dolina. "It's the weird things she has us at."

"Where's Mr. Gorman?"

"He'd the wee heart turn just after the New Year. He's not too serious, but they say he won't be coming back to the teaching."

The classroom was transformed – walls bright with pictures, in one corner a bookcase full of paperbacks, along one wall a table labelled FIND OUT FOR YOURSELF and covered with instruction packs. There was a nature table and a table with piles of paper, crayons, paint jars and sticky, coloured squares.

"Now, you'll be Jinny," welcomed Miss Broughton. "I've heard all about you. What would you like to do this morning? Write the story about your adventure on the moors?"

"What I'd really like to do," said Jinny, her voice squeaky with disbelief, "is to paint a picture of Shantih on the moors and the snow monsters."

"Fine," agreed Miss Broughton, "and after you've finished it, you can make up a sci-fi story with your monsters in it. Or a play?"

"I *must* be dreaming," Jinny said to Mike as they rode home. "There's no other explanation."

But if Jinny was dreaming, it went on through January and February and into March, as Shantih grew sleek and well again. Her chestnut coat was gleaming and supple and her silken mane and tail as fine as Jinny's own hair. By March, she was out during the day, sharing the same field as Punch and Bramble. When Jinny came home from school, Shantih was always waiting at the field gate, whinnying a welcome. If Jinny called from her bedroom window, the mare would look up from her grazing, searching for Jinny, then, seeing her at the window, would walk to the corner of the field nearest to the house and wait, watching her mistress. She had all the pure-bred Arab's magic, that note of brittle vulnerability mixed with the enchantment of a dream horse.

Jinny didn't want to start riding her until she was quite certain that Shantih was really fit again. She led her about in a halter – down to the farm, along the road to Glenbost, over the moors and along the shore. All her fear of humans had vanished. It was only if she got a fright that she would rear away, as sudden and wild as she had been on the moors.

Then, one evening at the end of March, Jinny was walking back with the milk. The air was gentle and warm. Buds furred the etched branches of the trees, a flush of green grass tinted the moors, and suddenly Jinny knew that it was the right time to start riding Shantih.

The next evening she adjusted Bramble's bridle and went down to the field. Shantih came trotting to the gate.

"Going to ride you tonight," said Jinny. "How will that be?"

The mare pushed her soft velvet muzzle into the crook of Jinny's arm. Jinny scratched her behind the ears, flipped stray locks of mane over to the right side of her neck, and very gently lowered the reins over her head. Then she slipped the thick snaffle into Shantih's mouth and lifted the bridle over her ears. When she had buckled the throat lash and noseband, Jinny gathered up her reins and gently, talking all the time to the mare, she lay over her withers.

Shantih stood quite still, hardly paying any attention to Jinny, relaxed and easy. Jinny slid her arms round Shantih's neck.

"Whoa, the lass. The good horse. Steady now, easy the girl." Slowly and carefully, Jinny lifted her leg over Shantih's back and sat astride her.

Shantih turned an enquiring head, nibbled at the toe of Jinny's sandshoe, asking what all the fuss was about.

Jinny touched her legs against Shantih's sides and flexed her fingers on the reins, then Shantih was walking out with a gay willingness, her neck arched and proud, her dark, lustrous eyes looking around her as Jinny walked her in wide circles.

"You've got chestnut hairs all over the seat of your trousers," said her mother.

"I was riding Shantih," said Jinny. "She was perfect. Absolutely perfect."

Jinny hurried Bramble home from school the next afternoon. She was planning to ride Shantih along the road to Glenbost. As Bramble passed the farm gate, he stopped suddenly and gave one of his trumpetting whinnies. A chorus of shrill neighs replied, and Jinny realised that the Shetlands must be in the paddock. She rode Bramble across the farmyard to have a look at them. She hadn't really seen them since the blizzard.

"Aye," said Mr. MacKenzie, who was leaning on the gate, ruminating over his ponies. "It's yourself."

"They're looking well," said Jinny.

"No bad," agreed Mr. MacKenzie. "The yearlings will be off tomorrow. A wee touch pocket money that'll be."

"I was riding Shantih last night," Jinny said. "I'm going to ride her along the road to Glenbost tonight."

"That's obliging now," said Mr. MacKenzie. "Save me the trouble of coming to fetch her."

"What?"

"She'll be for the sale tomorrow," said Mr. MacKenzie, staring out over the shaggy mass of Shetlands.

"What do you mean – sale?"

"I told you long ago that I'd be taking her ladyship to the spring sale."

"But she's mine!" cried Jinny. "She's mine! I rescued her. I've looked after her. I've fed her. Shantih's MINE."

"Och now, enough of that nonsense. You know fine that I bought her from the circus man, and I've thrown in enough free hay and oats with the stuff your father's bought from me to keep two beasts, leave alone one scarecrow like her."

"You don't mean it?" demanded Jinny. "You can't mean it."

"That I do, lass. You can buy her from me for a hundred – and that's giving her away dirt cheap, seeing you've had so much going on with her."

"I haven't got a hundred pounds. Of course I haven't got a hundred pounds."

"In that case we'll say no more about it. Just you be bringing her over here tonight."

"Oh, please, please, Mr. MacKenzie, don't sell her. You can't sell her tomorrow. I'll find some way to make the money. Please."

The farmer turned away from Jinny. "Get off with you," he said gruffly, and stomped away into the farm.

Somehow Jinny rode Bramble back to Finmory. She couldn't cry. It was too bad for crying. She knew without asking that there was no chance of anyone giving her a hundred pounds. Not a chance in the world. Ken and Mr. Manders had re-established the pottery in one of Finmory's spare rooms and the shelves were filling up again, but they still hadn't made up for the pots they had lost in the gale. A publisher was interested in Mr. Manders' book, but he hadn't made a definite offer. There was nothing Jinny could do before tomorrow. Nothing. It was no use. All her struggling had been for nothing.

Clenched and desperate, Jinny turned Bramble out into the field. Shantih was at the gate but, after a quick glance, Jinny couldn't bear to look at her. She turned away and walked up to Finmory House. Its grey stone walls were enduring and strong. For so many years they had sheltered humans, all loving and hating, all powerless not to go on struggling. And in the end, it was no use. There was nothing you could do about anything. No matter how hard she tried not to, Jinny couldn't help seeing the red-gold shape of the Arab dancing in her mind's eye.

"Thought you were going to ride Shantih again tonight," her mother said, as Jinny walked into the kitchen.

Jinny shook her head.

"Mr. MacKenzie is going to sell her. Tomorrow at the sale. He wants a hundred pounds for her."

"Oh no! Did he tell you this just now?"

Jinny nodded, the lump in her throat choking her.

"I am sorry, pet, but we couldn't possibly."

"It's O.K.," gulped Jinny. "Didn't think you could." She fled out of the kitchen straight into Ken.

"Letter for you," he said.

Jinny took the letter. It was a large brown envelope with her name and address typed on it. She sat down on the bottom step of the stairs to open it, and pulled out a magazine.

"Who could have sent that to me?" Then she saw the letter. Her eyes pounced on it, devouring words – *"pleased to inform"* . . . *"judges"* . . . *"page 16"* . . . *"first prize"* . . . *"£60"*. She scrabbled the magazine open to page sixteen, and there was her competition painting, glossy and changed in its reproduction, and beside it was her name and address – winner of the first prize.

"Sixty pounds!" Jinny screamed, jumping to her feet. "I've won sixty pounds!"

She tore through to the kitchen, waving the magazine. "Look – my picture!" she yelled. "I've won sixty pounds."

"You've what?" said her mother, but Jinny was already tearing across the yard, running faster than she had ever run in her life before, her feet battering down the track to the farm.

Mr. MacKenzie was standing by the milking shed when Jinny arrived, too out of breath to speak. She could only hold the magazine open in front of him and point to her name.

"It's no a hundred," said Mr. MacKenzie, when he had

124

at last realised what Jinny was telling him, but she knew from his voice that he didn't mean it. "What about the other forty? Have you thought of that?"

"H.P.?" suggested Jinny.

"You painted this yourself now? Just you did it?"

"Yes."

"Well, you be doing me two of the farm and we'll call it a deal."

Jinny threw her arms around his neck and kissed him.

She went back to Finmory, walking slowly, joy singing and bursting out of her.

"You're mine now. Truly mine," she told Shantih as she put her bridle on. She led the Arab out of the field, sprang lightly on to her back and rode her down the path to the bay.

"It's all beginning," Jinny said aloud. "An Arab of my own to ride, to train and to love."

The freedom of the craggy moors and the open sea stretched around Jinny. She ran her hand down Shantih's strong, sleek neck as the mare walked out with an even, reaching stride, her ears flickering to the sound of Jinny's voice. Long summer days lay ahead of them both, when they would ride together far into the hills, discovering hidden lochs and secret beaches, but always the strong, grey walls of Finmory House would be there – waiting to welcome them home again.

"I do love you," Jinny said, meaning not only Shantih but Finmory and her family and Ken; the hills and the sea; not only the soaring delight of the eagles but the insects as well. "I love you all so much."

And she sat astride Shantih, laughing for sheer joy. It was all possible now.

THE SILVER BRUMBY SERIES

ELYNE MITCHELL

Brumbies are the wild horses of Australia, hunted by man to be tamed for his own use. These six stories tell of Thowra, the Silver Brumby, and Kunama, his daughter, Wirramirra, his son, and Baringa, his grandson.

'These Brumby books are in a class by themselves . . . the horselover's dream' *Noel Steatfeild*

SILVER BRUMBY
SILVER BRUMBY'S DAUGHTER
SILVER BRUMBIES OF THE SOUTH
SILVER BRUMBY KINGDOM
SILVER BRUMBY WHIRLWIND
SON OF THE WHIRLWIND

ARMADA

'JINNY' BOOKS
by Patricia Leitch

When Jinny Manders rescues Shantih, a chestnut Arab, from a cruel circus, her dreams of owning a horse of her own seem to come true. But Shantih is wild and unrideable.

This is an exciting and moving series of books about a very special relationship between a girl and a magnificent horse.

FOR LOVE OF A HORSE
A DEVIL TO RIDE
THE SUMMER RIDERS
NIGHT OF THE RED HORSE
GALLOP TO THE HILLS
HORSE IN A MILLION
THE MAGIC PONY
RIDE LIKE THE WIND
CHESTNUT GOLD
JUMP FOR THE MOON
HORSE OF FIRE

Armada